THE SLEEPING LAND

A NOVEL

ELLA ALEXANDER

THE UNNAMED PRESS
LOS ANGELES, CA

AN UNNAMED PRESS BOOK

Published in North America by the Unnamed Press.

www.unnamedpress.com

Unnamed Press, and the colophon, are registered trademarks of Unnamed Media LLC.

Hardcover ISBN: 978-1-961884-19-9
EBook ISBN: 978-1-961884-33-5

Cover Design and Typeset by Jaya Nicely

Manufactured in the United States of America by Sheridan

Distributed by Publishers Group West

First Edition

To Mom and Dad,

who taught me to love people by trying to understand them

And there's a mighty judgment coming,
But I may be wrong.

—Leonard Cohen, "Tower of Song"

THE SLEEPING LAND

JUNE 1994

1

"We should have stopped inventing things after dogs," said Val, once she'd drunk enough. She had barely touched her dinner, a meat dish ordered in ignorance that had arrived minced nearly into plasma. The menu was given in Russian and French, but she had only a sparse, grammarless knowledge of each language. Even if she'd been able to read its meticulous wine list and varieties of caviar listed by color, she wouldn't really have understood.

All around her were rich people, rich foods, rich textiles. Red-faced businessmen newly wealthy from imports and government contracts; stately old party officials chewing morosely, giving off the perverse impression of aristocracy in exile; big wives in heirloom furs; little mistresses in Versace silk—none of whom made any attempt to hide their amusement at the mismatched newcomers. The candlelight was generous but shifting; heavy scents of butter, anise, and perfume hung about the room. Every detail seemed to have a secret meaning. But that was the way with all displays of culture, and she could steel herself against their judgment by taking an anthropological view.

The meat dish was harder to combat. She'd picked it because it was the second least expensive item on the menu. Her graduate thesis adviser, Dr. George Auberon, was paying for her meal along with those of her classmates, Mark Auchmill and Kit Lai. George would have noticed if she'd picked the cheapest option, as he noticed now that her meal was uneaten. But even the risk of offending George was not a great enough incentive to finish the meat paste. With an empty stomach, exhausted from the flight, unnerved by the trials of fine dining, she got drunk quickly.

"I mean, we should have made a conscious choice, as a species, to stop. Agriculture. Did that make us any happier? The wheel? Or . . . I don't know?" She motioned around her at the interior of the restaurant, candlelit with gilt-edged china and brocade tablecloths.

They'd landed in Moscow that afternoon. In the morning they were set to board the Rossiya north to Siberia, to excavate a cave inhabited throughout the paleolithic era, so George took the team out to dinner at a little place he knew in Rublevka for a last taste of civilization. The little place had turned out to be a Michelin star restaurant with an imported French chef, a menu of horse, lamb, duck, and rabbit. This was not entirely surprising. Val knew George's tastes well enough to pack a silky black dress along with her camping gear and excavation tools, and Kit always liked to dress for a nice dinner, but Mark had to be given a sports coat and tie from the restaurant's closet before the maître d' would let him in. The jacket, though of a high-quality charcoal wool, strained against his shoulders and clashed with his navy slacks. Val even felt a little bad for him.

"Really, besides dogs, I can't think of anything else about this I'd like to keep."

"Books?" Kit asked absently. She knew he was humoring her. He'd heard this speech before. "Art? Medicine?"

"Medicine, no. You see the way they string these poor old people along? Let them die. It's grotesque, these nursing homes, life support. But I guess that's the price. The march of progress. Progress toward what? But really, carving the wheel, how could we have known?"

"You'd rather be living in a cave then?" asked Mark. He had been an Eagle Scout and acted as if this made him more practical than the rest of them. In a way, he was right. She'd heard various stories about George's years in the field: that he'd spent ten months traveling with North Asian nomads, learning about sacred sites both active and abandoned; that he had a photographic memory and could wander freely through the Siberian tundra without ever getting lost; that he'd talked his way out of KGB detention and even—though he never alluded to this himself and she didn't quite believe it—that he'd killed a man once in self-defense. But she and Kit had both grown up in the suburbs of Toronto and would fare poorly in a paleolithic survival scenario.

"Yes."

"You wouldn't really. You can't even make a fire."

"Not me *now*. I mean if I could go back to infancy and do it over, you know?"

"It's stupid. You could die of a broken leg." Mark adjusted his dinner jacket, though the act did little good. No amount of willpower would make it fit properly. Val watched his struggle impassively. The rest of them—George, Kit, and herself—might have been taken for a family if you blurred your vision: black hair, black eyes, straight backs under black clothes. A certain dignity to all of them. Mark, in this family, would be what her father called the "redheaded stepchild." He really did have red hair. It was the first thing anybody noticed about him. Or one of the first things. Simultaneously, a person might notice that he was gigantic—six foot five with broad shoulders and blunt, heavy limbs. His clothing was worn out, wrinkled, seemingly picked at random from a laundry pile, and his voice was deep without richness. He'd asked her on a date in their first semester of grad school, and they'd disliked each other since.

"Well," said Val, "you could be hit by a taxi as soon as we leave the restaurant."

"I look before I cross the street."

"Maybe it's the taxi driver from *Taxi Driver*."

"Café? Dessert?" Their waiter had arrived again. He spoke in clipped French, addressing George exclusively.

"He doesn't hit anyone with the taxi in *Taxi Driver.*"

"But he could have. I wouldn't put it past him."

"Café, pour la table," said George.

"None for me," said Kit. He'd been moody since they met up at the airport, and there was no point in trying to cheer him up. At the start of dinner, he'd refused wine too, but George had insisted and asked him to make a toast.

"To life," he'd said, holding up his glass reluctantly. The wine was a bitter red that clung to the teeth. A very fine vintage, according to George.

"To life? Surely we can do better than that."

"Better than life?"

"To a successful expedition," Mark said.

They had clinked glasses quickly and in silence, unsure what they were toasting to, and drank their blood wine. Val gave Kit a questioning look, which he ignored. He began to engage only when George mentioned, quite casually, that the Sakha nomads believed that the Malova Valley, where they were going to dig, was haunted.

Val had laughed, delighted. Mark looked more alarmed but, in a show of both strength and deference, said that perhaps the Sakha were responding to a sudden shift in altitude. Human beings were very sensitive to atmospheric conditions, even if they don't realize it consciously. Kit asked George to elaborate.

"The Sakha place importance on natural balance, and the area where we're conducting our research is said to be *un*balanced." He poured himself more wine and twirled his glass around with a subtle motion of the elbow, his wrist unmoving. The wine circled his glass as evenly as if a drain sat at its center. His hand was gentle around the stem, his fingers long and thin, a signet ring glinting gold in the candlelight. Mark tried to imitate the movement, but he twitched his wrist so erratically that the liquid seemed to jump.

"That's not quite the same as haunted," said Kit.

"They say that hunters go missing there."

"A person could go missing in the Siberian winter easily," Mark reasoned. "Get lost. Freeze to death. And this happens a couple times in the same place, and suddenly everyone's sure there's an evil spirit."

"But it would have been nice to have learned this information before we flew out to Moscow," said Kit. And everybody laughed, although he wasn't joking.

In her hotel room that night, Val slipped off her dress in the dark, fell onto the full bed, and laughed. She had seventy dollars in her bank account, and her apartment lease would expire two weeks after the end of the dig. She was lying to everybody about her progress on her thesis. It was supposed to comment on prehistoric migration patterns through recurring and mutating motifs in cave art, though so far she'd only looked at slides now overdue at the university library. She'd made a fool of herself in front of George, argued with Mark all night, and spilled a drop of wine on her nicest dress—rayon, but it passed for silk in the candlelight. She rolled over onto her stomach and said aloud, "Well. Oh, well."

The walls were thin, and she could hear somebody pacing in the room next door.

2

THEY ARRIVED AT YAROSLAVSKY STATION EARLY IN THE morning, as the sun was rising. It was an old imperial building with a great arc of an entrance underneath a palatial roof. This was topped with what looked at first to be a gigantic wrought-iron tiara with a hammer and sickle grafted to the center. Inside, the high ceilings caused a draft to nip at their legs and an echo to follow their footsteps. Around them stood a scene of ruined splendor, twice over: chipped plaster moldings from the age of the czars, dull linoleum flooring from the sixties, black marble columns accented with gold, stark murals of soldiers and laborers. The halls were largely empty, besides a few cart vendors setting out the day's newspapers, a napping vagrant, and a trickle of weary travelers. A church-like expectation of silence was generally understood. They passed through the building and onto the platform, where the Rossiya was waiting for them, a faded red train with blocky white Cyrillic lettering running down its flank.

The interior of the train had been refurbished in plastics and polyester sometime in the 1970s, though these were now scratched and stained, graffiti carved into the tables, dents on every metal edge. Val could still see the attempt at a bright, clean, modern decorating scheme. The imagined future of a hopeful past. Val entered with Mark, after a porter separated them from the others. Kit and George had both paid extra for first-class tickets, and now she was trapped in a four-person sleeper compartment with a person who seemed both to hate her and to go out of his way to engage her in conversation. But after she declined his help with her duffel bag, he sat down silently with a book.

The train *choo*-ed as its wheels began to turn, like in an old cartoon. She'd had two cups of coffee and no food, which gave a hypoglycemic thrill to these first creaky movements. Soon it began to glide. She looked out the window at a sky dyed gray by either fog or pollution, then down at the dregs of outer Moscow, sliding into suburbs, farms, evergreen forests not unlike the one she'd spend the next six weeks in.

Nature made Val nervous. She had no fond memories of family hikes or camping trips, only an urban suspicion of depopulated places. This wasn't an ideal mindset for an archaeologist, and she kept it to herself. She liked action and variety, and often did unpleasant things just because they were interesting. And she loved the work. This seemed like enough to offset a lack of practical and spiritual connection with the natural world.

Besides, this was a wonderful opportunity. She and Kit kept repeating this to each other for days after they had been asked to go and again before their flight to Moscow. Kit, unexpectedly, was a nervous flier, and he'd babbled about the good this could do for his career for twenty minutes as the plane sat stalled on the runway, quieting abruptly when it began to taxi again.

It would be the first extensive Western dig on Russian soil since the execution of the czar, though not for a lack of interest. The University of California had applied to dig in Siberia two years ago, just months after the collapse of the Soviet Union, but its application to the Bureau of Land Management had been lost in the chaos of government restructuring and then promptly denied upon resubmission. Further inquiries were met with form letters.

George had seen a copy of the Americans' grant proposal from a colleague on sabbatical, and he later told Val he was not surprised by the rejection. The California dig had been part of the larger, multipronged Russo-American Academic Freedom Project, encompassing the fields of economics, journalism, physics, anthropology, and archaeology. Though this endeavor claimed to promote peace and unity, its constant mentions of "the free marketplace of ideas" and "developing the voice of a newly uncensored Russian people" gave the impression of a blood-coated warrior parading through the streets of a conquered land with the severed head of its king.

A too-complete faith in liberty's reach had been their downfall. Nobody in the newly formed Russian Federation's government had bothered, in the end, to replace the gray apparatchik in charge of archaeological excavation permits, and if the Americans had listed even half as many inalienable rights in their Russian application as they had in their grant proposal, the apparatchik could never have had as much pleasure in denying a permit as he had the day he thwarted the Russo-American Academic Freedom Project, or at least the archaeological wing of it.

George's own proposal was more modest. He would bring over a small group of graduate students for preliminary digs in a cave he'd noted as significant during one of his land surveys in the eighties. From there, if the site proved rich enough, battalions of unpaid Russian and Canadian undergrads would be sent for more thorough excavations. Though this seemed simple enough, George had been planning it for years. He'd told Val the whole story once at the faculty Christmas party, trying to look occupied to avoid talking to the head of the department.

He had been fascinated by Russia since childhood, by the land as much as the people. Like many boys, he'd liked military history and found it fascinating how the land had done as much to repel Russia's enemies as its soldiers. It was the land—hard, cold, incomprehensibly vast—that had ground down the armies of Napoleon and Hitler.

The forbidden status of the country drew him in too. He was born under cooling relations between East and West, and grew up through a string of narrowly avoided nuclear wars and hysterical rocket-building contests, atom spies, NATO, NORAD, Bond villains, ice hockey brawls between the Russian and Canadian teams. He felt this must be a strange and terrible place. And it was very unfair that he couldn't go see for himself.

His graduate thesis had been on totems in ice bridge cultures, with a focus on Alaskan artifacts, but his real interest lay across the Bering Strait. In the early years of glasnost, he had lobbied extensively for a visa to the USSR to conduct his research, and through a combination of charm and persistence, he had eventually managed to attach himself to an archaeological land survey of Krasnoyarsk Krai, on the western border of Yakutia. But when he arrived, the Russians had little use for him. His penchant for silk ties and romantic notion of cultural relativism made him seem like a dilettante. They'd give him wrong times for meetings and sometimes openly ignored him when he spoke. As he was bound to travel with the survey, however, they dragged him along with them through tiny villages in the mid-Siberian Krasnoyarsk Krai.

This was agony for George. He was an ambitious person. Truly ambitious people often pretend to be more indifferent than they really are, because true ambition is disturbing. It's natural for a man to seek success, to do as well for himself as he can manage in order to live a socially and materially comfortable life. But to value a vocation over love and money, people and objects—this is unnatural and untrustworthy. It singles you out; a trait that would get you killed in the Spanish inquisition, the Salem witch trials, Stalin's purges. George, luckily, had charm, so he didn't need to pretend as much. "I would have sold my soul to the devil," he told Val, "except the achievement wouldn't count that way."

"The closest thing most people experience to burning ambition is the painful pursuit of romantic love," he'd said later on in the night. "And in a way, ambition is a perversion of love. But the pain of love passes quickly. Ambition does not."

After months of fake smiles and cheery ploys, of being transferred through a maze of bureaucracy, he had finally acquired his golden visa only to be met with contempt. This caused his ambition to burn inward, to burn him up.

George picked languages up easily and had learned the basics of a number of Turkic tongues before applying to the survey. His job, ostensibly, had been to inquire among the Buryat villagers and nomads about possible man-made geographic features—funeral mounds and religious sites and the like—that they'd encountered in the area. He did ask this in each village, and while they told him nothing, the Buryats usually let him hang around until the survey dragged him away.

George's discipline, which he'd thought of as an integral part of his personality, began to slip. He spent most of his time drinking vodka, home-brewed beer, or a beverage made from fermented mare's milk called "tarasun." This last drink was used only for ceremonies and special occasions, but the land survey took place during the summer, and there always seemed to be a wedding or a birth or some seasonal holiday to justify it. It was one of the most alcoholic drinks known to man and caused occasional hallucinations.

Most Buryat villagers tolerated him when he came to drink with them. He brought interesting gifts, understood when to be unobtrusive, and picked up some basic vocabulary pretty quickly. He also had a remarkable talent, displayed only when drunk, for shadow puppets. He moved very quickly to form different creatures and, through rapid alternations, could create whole scenes by firelight: howling wolves, tigers eating rabbits, hawks descending upon hapless turtles. The sun set late and the nights were very brief, but often a few men stayed up long enough to goad him into one of these performances.

It was after one of these nights, among a group of nomads, that he woke up hungover and alone on the floor of a yurt, forty miles in the opposite direction from the Soviet land survey. They had moved twenty miles to the south that day, and he, without any memory of it, had gone twenty to the north. He stayed on with these Buryat nomads, and they allowed it for a while. Some of them grew to like him, with a few young men in a nomadic group becoming particular friends.

The survey was supposed to last ten weeks, owing to the exceptional size of the area they were attempting to map. He broke with them on the sixth week and did not attempt to rejoin the group. Had he thought the thing through more, he could have returned to Canada a month later and pronounced himself a leading North American expert on Siberian archaeology. None of the Russians would have bothered to contradict him. Admitting they'd lost him would involve a mountain of paperwork. But he had the misfortune of caring about his vocation, an irrational foundation leading to irrational action. He stayed in Russia to find what he'd been looking for on his own.

The Buryats were soon disenchanted with George. They found him useless at the work of everyday life. And, he conceded, he really was rather useless as a young man. George moved on ahead of them eastward and into Yakutia with rekindled ambition, and found things to be more promising. There, he met with the Yakuts, and a certain young widow who didn't care how useless he was in the daytime. She gave him a lot of useful information and let him stay with her as her group, who liked him less, traveled through grasslands and tundra. He won them over a little with the shadow puppets, and by the end of his first trip, he'd marked out a few solid points of interest throughout the region.

He returned to Yakutia a number of times. His overstay was forgiven through the intervention of government contacts, and subsequent visas proved easier to acquire than the first. He spent these trips learning the land, noting down certain unusual features he felt no responsibility to report. The collapse of the Soviet Union helped his plans along, but Val felt certain that he would have accomplished them even without the convenience of political upheaval. There are certain people around whom the world bends.

Mark's book was slim, a laminated paperback with a Roman bust on the cover. He'd bought it for an undergrad survey course and left it untouched until now. The packing list that George had sent them two months before included a number of highly specific and expensive items, including an ultralight sleeping bag, 50 DEET bug spray, and clothes in quick-drying fabrics ("Lycra or linen"), which felt like a test. Are you a Lycra man or a linen man? (Even so, Mark couldn't bring himself to buy new linen clothes on his stipend.) George's list ended with the thoughtful but ominous item: "Copious reading material. Conversation only goes so far!"

He had always loved to read. *I, Claudius*; the Hornblower novels; and, to reread annually, the *Lord of the Rings* trilogy. But these did not seem appropriate for Siberia, or at least not for Siberia with Dr. George Auberon, Kit Lai, and Valerie Howe. Instead, he brought *The Meditations of Marcus Aurelius*, *Moby-Dick*, *Howl and Other Poems*, *Life during Wartime: An Oral History of the Cambodian Civil War*, and a biography of Joseph Stalin with the lone word *STALIN* splayed in white letters across the black cover. This was a book that Mark, who liked modern history generally, had been trying to read for years with little success. He skipped the thirty-two-page introduction with every attempt, but its first chapter, tracing the Hellenistic roots of serfdom in Stalin's native Georgia, always defeated him. *STALIN* weighed five pounds, with the dimensions of a lunch box and pages as thin as a Bible's. *The Complete Lovecraft* was the only book he actually enjoyed that he'd decided to bring, but he wanted to save it, so he picked *The Meditations* to read first because it looked serious and also short.

He held it up high enough that Valerie could see the cover, but she didn't look over until he set the book down with a sigh to look out the window at a blur of pines. In his peripheral vision, he saw her glance down to read the title.

"*The Meditations*," he explained. He'd skimmed the first twenty or so pages, as he often did, because people looked trivial reading the first pages of a book in public. Still, he'd gotten the general thrust. "He was the original Stoic. Always expect the worst. Imagine it down to the details."

"I do that already."

"Me too. Everybody does it. But the point is to do it on purpose. To fortify yourself against fate."

Valerie nodded, smiled without teeth, and turned back to her own book, a novel called *Howards End*, which he had seen before in some context and vaguely associated with homosexuals. She was always slighting him like this. There was something in her smile that seemed calculated to wound. Nobody else seemed to notice it.

The economy-class dining car smelled of nicotine, beef stew, and unwashed skin. Its furniture was all plastic, in a playground color scheme of blue and orange. An orange-counter bar took up the left side, where a pair of Lacoste-clad Russians were happily downing shots on blue barstools while a bloated American in an unironed shirt loudly explained how to count cards to the miserable Mongolian bartender. A Chinese businessman sat alone in a booth with an untouched plate of eggs, writing a list in hanzi on a legal pad, and a haggard mother tried to soothe her whining baby behind him. A herd of young backpackers took up two booths without ordering anything. They were occupied with rolling cigarettes, trying to find a lost coin on the floor (a three-man operation), and bickering in French over a map of Eurasia. One of them kept holding her Polaroid camera up to the window and snapping pictures of the trees. "Merde," she'd say, shaking each developing photo. "C'est floue."

The only empty booth had puddles of sweat on both benches, but there were two free barstools between the card counter and the Russians. Val, who had come to the dining car only to get away from Mark and Marcus Aurelius, sat herself next to the Russians. The bartender came over quickly to greet her, abandoning the card counter in the middle of a story he was telling about sneaking back into the Casino de Monte-Carlo with a fake beard after a ban. She asked for hot chocolate and an éclair from the glass cake dome in the corner by the Russians. As the bartender, with his back conspicuously turned away from his patrons, took agonizing pains with the ratio of cocoa to milk in a metal cup, the card counter turned to Val. He stared at her for a moment without saying anything while she watched the bartender mixing milk and powder with a resolute focus.

"Thought you were a boy," said the card counter.

Val did not reply. He'd heard her order, though, and knew she spoke English.

"I thought you were a boy," the card counter said again, louder.

"Well," said Val, as she received her drink. She tried to make eye contact with the bartender, but he ignored her.

"Why do girls do that?" the man asked. "Cut their hair like that?"

Val shrugged.

"I suppose you're a backpacker then," he continued, with increasing disdain. "Trying to see the world? To find yourself?"

"Yeah," said Val. This was a terrible turn, escaping Mark only to be met with this drunker, less intelligent antagonist.

"I'm here on business, believe it or not."

"With the cards?"

"That's a side thing," he said, with a wave of his hand. "I make deals. Business. For, well, I shouldn't say who. For interested parties."

She nodded slightly, having no response to this and understanding that none was expected.

"But I can let you in on one secret," he said, lowering the tone, though not the volume, of his voice. "Siberia." He gestured behind them at the blur of trees that the French girl was still attempting to photograph. They hadn't yet reached the region's western edge, but the trees were probably similar enough here as there to the untrained eye. "Worthless, right? Coldest place in the world in the winter. Nothing alive but pines and wolves and Eskimos. But in ten, fifteen years, it's gonna be the most fertile farmland in the world." He paused for emphasis. "You know why?" Another pause. This lasted long enough that she realized he actually wanted her to ask.

"Why?"

"Greenhouse gases. We're gonna buy this shit up, pennies on the mile, then come the twenty-first century, the new millennium, we'll be rolling in it. My clients? Richest guys in the world in, say, 2012."

"What if they stop it? Solve the greenhouse gases?"

The man laughed. "*They?* They who? *They* don't give a *fuck*."

She wondered if she might pretend to know the French backpackers. Would they play along? How much French could she manage? She hadn't paid much attention in high school but had taken three compulsory years of the language. *Bonjour, mes amis.* But then, in this moment of crisis, she couldn't remember anything except for the names of foods.

"Say, what's your name?" asked the man.

Saucisson. Pomme de terre. Haricots verts. Merde, c'est floue. "I'm Diana."

"Lady Di! Doug." He extended a greasy hand. His pinkie nail, she noticed, was disturbingly long, stained yellow by nicotine. As he shook her hand, it dug into her palm. What now? She would just say she had a headache and leave. Mark was more tolerable than this. And she had a walk of three train cars to fortify herself against fate. But then, like an angel sent by a merciful god, Kit appeared. Without saying anything, he waited for her at the end of the bar, behind the Russians.

"Who's your new friend?" Kit asked, once they'd reached the safety of the next car, a long hallway full of mostly empty suites.

Val laughed. "Doug. He says this is going to be the most fertile farmland in the world in the twenty-first century."

"I trust him."

"Thanks for saving me."

"I was looking for you. Mark said you'd gone to the dining car."

Val fished through her canvas tote bag until she came up with a pack of Marlboros. Whenever Kit sought her out, he wanted a smoke. When they first met, he would always try to come up with some sort of pretense to talk to her before asking, but now he'd just wait for her to offer.

Out of everyone on the expedition, Val felt most comfortable with Kit. Strategically quiet and strikingly handsome in pressed shirts and Italian shoes, his black hair styled with pomade and a fine-tooth comb like an old movie star's, he had the opposite effect on most people. He didn't make much effort to reassure them either. Classmates and even professors would stiffen while talking to him, laugh nervously, qualify and second-guess every statement, although he never corrected them.

But Val was used to bad company and respected his indifference to other people's discomfort. They'd been assigned a group project together, along with an exuberant divorcée reclaiming her life and passions after a decade of domestic servitude, whom Val felt guilty for disliking. Allied by circumstance against their group mate's optimism, she and Kit had immediately started up a rapport of startling honesty combined with a complete lack of interest in each other's personal lives. This carried them through their presentation on pottery sherds in different Köppen climates in spite of the divorcée's attempts to corner them into meaningful conversations about their hopes and dreams, near-death experiences, Jungian analysis, *You Can Heal Your Life*, and the Buddha. They'd been friends since, but not the sort who met off campus.

She appreciated him mainly as a judge of character. They would analyze people together, which differed from gossip in that it concerned itself with unconscious motives. Kit was harsher than Val in his estimates, but it was rare to find another person who paid attention at all, and she liked to compare notes. Otherwise, she interacted with him in her usual way with male friends: sarcastic, disinterested, with no intimate disclosure made on either side except in the form of throwaway jokes. But it was easier with Kit, because he was married, with a new baby.

At first, this unnerved Val, that a person just three years older than herself could create and continuously nurture a family. Marriage and procreation, home ownership, it all felt too permanent and adult, an acknowledgment that their lives were terminable and decisions had to be made. "There is a natural arc to a life," Kit had said, on one of the rare occasions when he'd been willing to discuss it. "Most people know this intuitively."

The wife, Melissa, was a glossy-haired Korean Canadian trauma surgeon who would occasionally bring Kit lunch on her days off, greeting nobody and expecting those incidentals sitting near her husband to make their excuses and clear away, which, inevitably, they did. Val had finally spoken to her at the last faculty Christmas party. Melissa, seven months pregnant in an empire waist maroon brocade dress and kitten heels, had explained in between sips of seltzer that she played selections from *Don Giovanni* and *The Marriage of Figaro* to her stomach every night in order to stimulate development. Val had asked Kit about this later, whether the baby was supposed to come out screaming in scales, and had offended him so terribly that he'd walked away without a word. She'd had to grovel the next day, making jabs at her stunted and dysfunctional personal life, before he deigned to ask for a light. (She was, by then, used to his moods, although she had never caused one herself before. He was wonderful when he felt like being wonderful, but he would sometimes barely speak for days at a time before suddenly returning to himself without explanation or apology.)

Melissa was useful, though, because she removed any sexual tension from Val's interactions with Kit. Men and women could be friends, of course, but unless one of them happened to be gay or married, there was always a carnal possibility sitting between them, unspoken but never quite forgotten. With Kit, she could flirt as much as she wanted. Going home every night to his bone-setting, skin-grafting, well-groomed pillar of femininity, he saw Val more as a second cousin who drank too much at funerals but sometimes sold you pot when you felt like transgressing than, as George had once half jokingly called her, a modern Audrey Hepburn.

3

Sitting facing each other on the bed and leather ottoman in Kit's cabin, they quickly filled the small enclosure with smoke. He'd mostly sought her out for her company, having spent the morning restless and alone, mulling over problems he couldn't solve on this continent. But a cigarette couldn't hurt, especially without Min-Seo to go home to, telling him she could smell tobacco in his clothes.

"What was up with you last night?" asked Val.

"What do you mean?"

"You seemed annoyed, I don't know."

Kit exhaled, letting the nicotine relax his jaw. "I don't appreciate power games. Taking us to that place without even letting us know to dress up—"

"You were wearing a suit."

"—trying to force me to drink that black sludge."

"So you two haven't been sitting around in first class talking about how glad you are to be rid of me?"

"He's two doors down, but I heard him walk away half an hour ago."

Val laughed in disbelief. "You've been listening for his footsteps?"

"Only because he's been listening for mine. He tried to corner me in the hallway and *pick my brain.*"

"Why'd you come if you hate him so much? It's just gonna be us, him, and Mark."

"It's not summer holiday, Val. I didn't come for the company."

"Still. Six weeks alone in the tundra."

Not for the first time, they both considered this. "Christ," said Kit. "I think Mark's gonna snap and murder me. You'll come looking for us and find him in my tent wearing my peeled-off face as a mask."

"If anyone snaps, it'll be you." Having some sense of bookish male solidarity, he had sympathy for Mark, and the complete contempt in which Val held him sometimes bothered Kit. Even if he was occasionally obnoxious, he was handsome in a farmhand-ish way, intelligent, and certainly more tolerable than George. She never talked about her conquests, and he would have changed the subject if she tried, but he'd seen her brush her hand against George's arm, always with plausible deniability of course, and giggle like an idiot at his little asides about departmental politics.

He couldn't understand it. She had mentioned a dead mother and an erratic sister who read fortunes for a living in California, but seemed to have a pleasant twice-monthly phone call relationship with her father. Min-Seo disliked her. She said Val was one of those women who charmed men easily but couldn't weather hardship and would end up alone, volunteering at food banks just for the social interaction. "People find her charming?" he'd asked, to placate her. But now he pictured it sometimes: Val, old and withered in a sweater set, handing out Campbell's to young mothers in a church basement, grabbing on to their wrists and telling them to lock down their men while they still had their looks, then going home to a dirty apartment and a pack of decrepit shih tzus.

But this was unkind. Val was his friend, a generous one, and remarkably understanding when it came to him, at least.

"How's Melissa?" Val asked. This was the name Min-Seo went by professionally and the one she'd given to Kit's colleagues.

"Fine."

"With the baby?"

"She's having her mom come to help until I get back."

"Makes sense." Val stretched her legs and yawned. "I only have two left after these," she said, placing her hand over the wilted cigarette pack in her lap. "Then we're going to have to take our chances with the Russian smokes."

Val told him more about the drunken American gambler she'd been accosted by in the dining car and her theory that she could probably get cocaine off him if Kit was interested. He said it couldn't hurt to try and then, after she left, began a letter to his sensible, intelligent wife on his electric portable.

Dear Min-Seo,
I am writing to you from my cabin in the
Trans-Siberian, having left Moscow this morning.
You wouldn't believe how empty

Minnie,
Hey! I miss you already.

Min-Seo,
I hope

It would be better to wait until he had more to report. He'd called her from the hotel in Moscow, and all she wanted to talk about were practical details about communication and contingency plans in case of emergency that they'd already reviewed a dozen times. He'd said, "I love you . . ." with the drifting tone a person uses when trying to hang up, and she had asked if he'd like to speak to David.

"He can't talk."

"*You're* supposed to talk. So he doesn't forget your voice."

"Oh."

After they heard that she was having a baby, a number of Min-Seo's older male relatives had pulled him into the hallway at various gatherings to impart paternal advice. The first thing each old man told him was that he shouldn't worry if he didn't love his child at first. And, when he held David for the first time, he hadn't felt love, exactly, but rather a combination of fear, obligation, and wonder that might have been mistaken for love by a more sentimental or distracted parent.

After that first rush of emotion, he struggled to connect to the baby. David and Min-Seo seemed to disappear together into their own private communion, leaving him to wash the dishes and fold the laundry. He didn't want to be an absent father. He held his son, he bathed him, he warmed up his bottles and fed him, and he thought the whole time about his work.

Part of the problem had to be the name. It was ultimately ridiculous, he felt, for this baby to be called David. The name of a tribal king who had, three thousand years ago, ruled over a desert that his son, a North American born to two East Asians, would likely never see. There were tactical reasons for this choice. To avoid bad blood between the families, they couldn't really pick an overtly Chinese name or Korean one. Min-Seo said David had a good sound to it, with strength and definition. And people take on all sorts of names. His own name was fairly arbitrary.

People often asked him what it meant, and, not caring to explain Hong Kong naming practices to the Canadian public, he'd say he didn't know. His parents had chosen Kit pragmatically, because it sounded English enough to serve him in an Anglophone country and Chinese enough for China, or at least for Hong Kong. Of course, it sounded only and exactly like a Hong Kong baby-boom name. He'd been taunted in school with "kitty" and "Kit Kat" and variations of his name in fake Chinese gibberish rhymes, but he'd grown into it. At conferences, British people would sometimes assume it was short for "Christopher," which he sort of liked. He corrected them only when they got too comfortable and started to call him Chris. This was all much more trouble than David, without any added layers of symbol or tradition.

The real issue was that he couldn't think of his son—writhing, pink, covered in a layer of soft down hair—as anything but an animal, a creature of instinct that had no use for a name. Inside him, he knew, were coils of DNA that would eventually reveal David's disposition, his likes and dislikes, the structure of his face. But now, larval, he was a secret to his father as much as to himself. Would they like each other? Would they have much to say to each other once David was grown? Min-Seo's mother took a picture of Kit as he first held his baby in the hospital. He was thinking, *Who are you?* and then, inexplicably, *Forgive me*. But in the photo, he just looked tired.

He paid his taxes: "Daddy loves you," "Daddy misses you," "You'll be so big when I get home," "Be nice to Mommy," "Daddy loves you" (again), "Bye-bye."

Min-Seo made her excuses to hang up. Long distance, costing them a fortune.

4

THE TRAIN STOPPED AT ANOTHER STATION THAT AFTERNOON. Val stepped off to buy some snacks at the newsstand on the platform: potato chips and a doughnut that turned out to be filled with minced pork. When she returned, a new passenger had joined Mark in their four-bed cabin. The man wore a shabby brown trench coat and smelled strongly of cologne. His face was strikingly ugly, with eyes widely set and round beneath a heavy brow, a blunt isosceles nose, his lower lip as fat as if he'd just staggered out from a bar brawl. He might have been forty or seventy and, without speaking, radiated a strained aura of malevolence. Val thought he looked like the mad German actor Klaus Kinski.

"Privyet," she said. The man only nodded at her, then began riffling through his large duffel bag until he found a pair of nail scissors. He spent an inordinate amount of time scraping dirt from underneath his fingernails and wiping it on the side of his bed as Val and Mark tried not to watch. Occasionally he would laugh at nothing and shake his head. By the time he left, for either the bathroom or the dining car, Val had begun to entertain the idea that he really *was* Klaus Kinski. She ran this theory by Mark, who had never heard of Kinski but still disagreed in the strongest terms. While more than half joking when she first brought it up, his vehemence made her double down.

"I wouldn't mistake a face like *that.*"

"What would Klaus Kinski be doing in an economy-class bunk on the Trans-Siberian?"

"He would do all sorts of things. You just said you didn't know him."

"Anyways, he's Russian, not German. I heard him speak when he first got on and you were out on the platform."

"In Russian?"

"Yeah."

"What did he say?"

"Well, in English, to me, he said hello, but the accent was Russian."

"He's an actor. He can do different voices."

"That's insane. Nobody does that."

"You've never even heard of him, and suddenly you're the expert?"

"It's all about probability. Do you even understand, statistically—"

"Strange things happen."

They went on like that until Kinski slid the door open and both immediately fell silent, pretending to read.

Val spent half an hour aimlessly pacing the halls. She walked into the dining car at some point, where Doug sat in his same seat at the bar, as if he'd never left. He spotted her immediately and smiled as if he was genuinely glad to see her. "Lady Di!"

She tried to walk through to the first-class cabins on the other side to see Kit, but a porter stopped her. Preferring the inexplicably menacing presence of Klaus Kinski to another installment in the saga of Doug's financial adventures, she returned to her cabin, where she found the madman adjusting Mark's Timex watch to fit his wrist.

"We were just playing cards," Mark explained, without looking at her. He was clicking a pen open and closed in his hand.

"Ha!" said Kinski.

Although it wasn't yet nine, Val climbed up to her top bunk and rolled over, pretending to sleep. She had a bag of potato chips stashed under her blanket, which she ate from in silence, putting each chip into her mouth and letting her saliva soften it into a mush before she swallowed. Her mouth burned with salt by the time she actually fell asleep, and she dreamed she was drinking from an ocean.

Val woke up to find that night had fallen. This far north, in the summer, the sun set after midnight. So she must have fallen deeply asleep without preparing for it. Her current disoriented state supported this. Still in her jeans, her hips felt sore where the metal rivets on her pockets had dug into them. Her mouth was terribly dry and still stung from the salt she'd sucked off her chips. The sound of the train's wheels against the track, which she'd barely noticed in the day, now grated on her ears.

When she rolled over, she saw Klaus Kinski standing in the middle of the cabin, his thick jaw slack, wide-set eyes glinting madly and fixed on the bunk below Val's, where Mark slept. After a pang of pure terror, she realized that he was sleepwalking. She'd seen the look before. Her sister, Lily, used to sleepwalk when they were kids, shuffling over to Val's bed, tugging on her arm, and whining, "Mooom, we're gonna be late!"

Val lay still for a minute, but when Kinski made no movements, she thought it would be safe to climb down, quietly, to retrieve her reusable water bottle. She didn't dare rouse the sleepwalker but wondered if she should try to wake Mark. Then, as she climbed barefoot down from her bunk, she saw that his eyes were already open. He looked desperately at her, and she shrugged. He was boxed in by the sleepwalker, with no way out. She wasn't sure what he wanted her to do. Kinski heard her feet touch the ground, or perhaps saw her in front of him—Val was never quite clear on the mechanics of sleepwalking—and lurched forward, grabbing on to her shoulders and whispering, "Mareike . . ." He stroked her hair with surprising tenderness, and she jumped backward, knocking her elbow against the door. She turned, slid the door open, and moved quickly into the hall. After walking quickly to the end of the car, she looked back to see that the madman had followed her out of the room and was standing bewildered behind her, only ten feet away.

The doors between the cars remained unlocked. Whether this was standard procedure or miraculous negligence, Val did not know. She hurried through the dark train, bare feet silent on the carpet, fingertips tracing the vibrating wall as she moved. The train at night was eerie, with mechanical clinks and shaking shadows. In the gangways between the cars, she could feel the cold wind rushing up from the gap between the two metal compartments. Hanging teacups tapped against one another to make a high, disorganized ringing sound in the dining car. Murder mysteries were often set in trains, she knew, though she'd never before considered why. Daylight brought with it a set of comfortable assumptions that allowed her to brush away the incomprehensible. At night, the train seemed to move faster and with less regularity, like an animal.

After stumbling through the dining car—walking straight into the bar, its sharp corner stabbing her in the gut—she passed finally into the first-class cars. Kit's light was off. She tried his door anyway, but he'd locked it, and attempting to wake him up would wake the whole hall. Farther on, she saw that George's light was on. It seeped out through the edges of his door like a halo. She put her ear to the door and heard the scratching of a pen through it. She tapped lightly on the door, and the scratching stopped. "George," she whispered.

No reply.

"George, it's Val."

After a moment, the door opened, and he ushered her in, looking disconcerted. All he said was "Hello."

She apologized and explained about the sleepwalking madman who'd stolen Mark's watch and called her Mareike. She spoke with manic animation, grateful to be away from Klaus Kinski and the ambiguous dark of the train. George had adopted an easy smile, now that he understood the situation.

"Don't laugh. It was really scary. His hand was so greasy he left oil in my hair when he touched it. Do you see?"

"It looks the same."

"Well, I feel it."

He told her to take a second to breathe and motioned for her to sit down in his chair, which still had his blazer draped over it. This being the same gesture he used when they met in his office, she sat quietly. The room, bathed in the warm light of the lamp, with creamy walls and dark wood furniture, felt more imperial than Soviet. George sat across from her, on his bed. He was still dressed in his day clothes, although it must have been past midnight. His feet were covered only by black socks, so worn that she could see the outline of his toenails under them. He'd lost a toe to frostbite early in his career, a fact she'd known for years now but had never before been able to confirm. But there it was, a strange, sudden dent. His pants, she thought, had been recently ironed. He'd placed a hand on his knee, and she noticed he still wore his signet ring. Maybe he never took it off, even to sleep. She couldn't bring herself to look at his face.

Instead, the desk: a lamp; an Olivetti typewriter; a half-folded topographical map purchased from some fastidious nation's military, thin as tissue; a box of cotton paper; a Montblanc pen loose next to its stand, rolling between the typewriter and the box of paper with the motion of the train; a Breguet watch; two small cups and a crystal decanter filled with whiskey. Did that come with the first-class cabins, or did he pack his own decanter? She hadn't noticed one on Kit's desk. He was in her line of sight again. He looked very tall beneath the train's low ceiling, easy, upright, and perfectly civilized. Apollonian, she had often thought. A professional.

He didn't actually need a job, coming from family money on his father's side. His mother had been connected to the Georgian royal family, a second or third cousin to the heir to the throne—everybody repeated this detail, although he himself never mentioned it. Val tended to believe it. Academics often had money coming in from unrelated sources. Usually this just meant a family-owned gas field or a grandfather on the board of the national bank, but a German countess had been granted tenure in the literature department and a younger son of the king of Lesotho studied at the graduate school for economics.

Even without this information, a person might call George's bearing aristocratic. He wore linen all through the summer, and it never seemed to wrinkle. It was hard to imagine him camping in the wilderness for weeks at a time, on his knees in muddy pits, scraping along the ground with a trowel. And yet, he'd been doing it for twenty years, hadn't he?

"So you left Mark?"

"What?"

"Mark? You left him with this Kinski character?"

"What was I supposed to do?" Her hands were shaking. She really had been startled.

George, standing at his desk, set the Montblanc right in its stand and poured out two glasses of whiskey. He handed one to her, not letting go until he was sure she had a good grasp on it. "To calm your nerves."

She took a sip. "He was awake, anyway, and he has a little Swiss Army knife."

This addition achieved the opposite of its intended effect, and George inquired as to whether they should check on him, or at least find a porter to assess the situation.

"I guess," she replied. She couldn't openly advocate for the abandonment of Mark, but felt entirely unwilling to leave the safety of the well-lit room.

"Has this man displayed any signs of violence?"

"No, he didn't really say anything to us."

George nodded. In a way it was touching, he reasoned, the strange man's midnight yearning for a lost love. He didn't seem angry with his Mareike, did he? There was no indication that he wanted to *harm* anybody. Val agreed.

George sat down again on the bed, which looked as if it had been remade a little carelessly. She wondered if he'd taken a nap that afternoon. He seemed like the sort of person who might have scheduled naps, with some sort of philosophical or historical justification for the practice, even if it really just stemmed from a habit of keeping strange hours.

"I'm really sorry about all this," she said, bringing the whiskey back to her lips. She was a nervous drinker, she knew, but now was not the time to check the habit.

"It's all right, really."

She should have offered to leave, to let him get some sleep, but didn't want to risk the chance that he might agree and send her off.

She probably couldn't stay all night. There was nowhere for her to sleep, and he'd want her out eventually, but she knew he wouldn't bring it up directly. He'd always been exceedingly polite to her, attentive to her comfort. With men, he could be competitive, even confrontational. Kit always clashed with him on small matters, though she'd never seen George maintain his rancor for as long as he seemed to be doing now. Something horrible had happened between him and the head of the department too. Somebody told her the head had given a talk on grain analysis in Algonquin mortars and pestles the year before, and George had raised his hand at the end and asked him if he hadn't sent these samples to a lab involved in a contamination scandal, run by his wife's uncle. But this seemed a little ridiculous.

With Val, he made a point of offering candied almonds when they met. He listened carefully to her ideas and paused to think before responding. His speech patterns revealed a remarkable clarity of mind; he was the only person Val had ever known who spoke almost entirely in fluid, grammatically correct sentences, like an audiobook. And his responses were always surprising. Kit said she was his favorite, and it was true that he consulted her first in meetings with his TAs, laughed more readily at her jokes, and had once inquired with real concern about whether she was getting enough to eat. But then, if she ever asked how he was doing in a tone that suggested sincerity, he'd turn cold, saying that he was very well, thank you, but busy.

"What were you working on?" This seemed safe and like it would take up at least some time.

"Oh, it's nothing."

"Letters?"

"I've been putting off reading some articles that *Archaeological Science* sent for me to review." His tone did not encourage further questioning.

"Well," she said, with increasing desperation, "the map . . . ?"

"The Malova Valley." He paused. She had to offer to leave. Perhaps she could take something as a weapon. "This site," he continued, "is giving me some trouble. I've hired a plane to get us there from Yakutsk, but I'm afraid the initial survey wasn't provided with the resources necessary for accuracy. I found the site on my own, you know. I flew up in a little Polikarpov, a biplane from World War Two—"

"*You* flew it?"

"I was half convinced it would fall from the sky—it made a sort of coughing noise when I started the engine. Keep in mind, I had no funding at this point, no backing from the university. The Polikarpov I rented from a farmer."

"But how did you learn to fly?"

"A biplane isn't difficult. The hard part was navigating the state bureaucracy. Even with glasnost, it was hell getting the Soviets to grant my visa. They were convinced I was working for the Americans, feeding information to the CIA."

"You? A professor?"

"Ten years earlier, they'd uncovered an American-French plot to free dissidents from a Siberian prison camp under the guise of an archaeological survey, and they suspected a repeat, I think. But I had no notion of this at the time. Even after the visa was somehow approved, they pulled me aside in the airport and asked me all sorts of questions about my political leanings, my national loyalties, my family ties. The interrogator brought up an article I'd coauthored in grad school about possible economic systems in neolithic Anatolia." Remembering this, he laughed. "Would you like another drink?"

"Thank you."

He poured one for her and one for himself.

"Do you always stay up this late?" she asked.

"I don't seem to need as much sleep as other people."

"That's lucky."

"It's useful in Siberia, I've found. We'll have twenty-one hours of daylight in Yakutia."

"I brought an eye mask." She looked out the window. It was snowing, softly. They were officially in Siberia now, and she'd heard this could happen here occasionally, even in early summer. Snowflakes hit the window and melted on contact.

"Would you mind looking over something with me?"

He rose and walked over to join her by the desk. She stood: five feet tall, jeans uncuffed, dragging against the floor and hiding her feet nearly to the toes. She felt like a child. "Have you recovered?" he asked, as he reached for the topographical map and unfolded it in midair. She wasn't sure if he was teasing her, so just nodded.

The lamplight glowed through the map as he unfolded it, illuminating rivers and streams like veins beneath living skin. The map fluttered as he pulled it down toward the desk. The life dimmed and, as it hit the wood, died.

"You'd be better off asking Kit a geographical question."

George waved this idea away with his long-fingered hand. "It's not a geographical question. More psychological. I asked some Sakha about any carvings, paintings, man-made anomalies in the area that didn't come from them. They told me about a cave in the shape of a bear's mouth by the Lena River. They said it was a place where people had always been. Nobody would take me there, but I found something fitting the description."

He pointed, on the map, to a little red dot he'd added. "But these maps are never as accurate as you might hope. I communicated with the Sakha in Russian, so there was some difficulty there too. My Sakha is passable in a casual context, but not for research matters. And Nyurgun's Russian was shaky. He had trouble with the noun genders and so entirely dispensed with plurals."

"Oh."

"Nyurgun is the man who first told me about the cave, and I located the most likely site through a combination of aerial and ground survey. But the issue is, I think there might be a second significant cave. He said the cave was 'colored'—that's a direct translation—and there's nothing to indicate that our cave fits that description."

"I see." She was still waiting for a question she wasn't qualified to answer. But he seemed to have forgotten that he'd asked for her help, and the question never came.

"Don't mention this to the others. Kit is attached to procedure."

"Do you think so?"

"He has his ideas, in any case. As for Mark, he's very intelligent, but he sometimes misses the forest for the trees."

"He's pedantic."

"It's insecurity, I think, from his upbringing." Mark came from a rural town, which he mentioned only occasionally, with sharp bitterness. He was even poorer than Val, who at least had a father with a pension and a sense of obligation.

"His parents are second cousins, you know."

"That's not unusual. My mother's parents were cousins."

Cousin marriage, the cause uniting displaced aristocrats and the rural poor. "I didn't mean it as a bad thing, just something I heard."

She turned her head back to the map, trying to look studious.

The dot, George explained, was the location of their cave, but if she could picture the actual geographical features depicted and imagine herself to be in this wilderness, searching for shelter, would this really be her first option?

"It's not unlikely that activity occurred in this cave—I'm certain it did—but would it really be a site of consistent habitation?"

Val considered this. "It's a bit of a climb. But maybe that was good. Added protection. But it's hard to picture, really. It reminds me of Oskolkina cave, almost." This was a ritual site in the Altai Krai that George had told her to study.

He nodded and rolled the map up. "It'll be easier, of course, to gauge that once we get there."

She looked at him. His face stayed grave, but with light behind the eyes.

She'd first taken a class with him as an undergrad, an introductory survey course with 150 students in a newly built amphitheater. On the first day, he'd passed ancient pottery sherds around the room and told the students to run their hands along the grooves in the clay. These were made, he said, by fingerprints, by the unique marks in the skin of people who lived thousands of years ago. And now you're touching them, running over these grooves with your own fingerprints. A direct link through time.

At the end of the semester, Val had switched her major from English literature to archaeology. With so many students, he probably didn't remember she'd been in that class. *Thank you,* she wanted to tell him, *for the only sincere thing in my life.*

"Look," she said instead, pointing to the window. The snow had stopped falling, and now it seemed to impose a stillness on the ground it covered, a surreal, suspended quality that sapped any desire to speak or think in the mundane way that people spoke and thought about their own circumstances. It was human nature to love fresh snow, the alien blankness of it, the way it erased the world, lifted the weight of context. And then the satisfaction of stepping in it, soiling it, pushing through to the dirt as if you were the first person to ever walk the earth, prehistoric, gigantic, alone. It felt wrong that she couldn't walk through the snow now, that she was cut off from it. But its glow was only a reflection of the light of the moon, she knew, which itself was reflecting the light of the sun. An echo of an echo.

George looked too. After a moment he remarked that it was already starting to melt.

5

George wouldn't hear of her returning to the clutches of Klaus Kinski and insisted that she get at least a few hours of sleep in his bed while he typed up some notes. He did just that, typing at a good pace and ignoring her entirely. She could smell his shampoo on the pillow when she laid down her head, but she fell asleep quickly and woke up early, refreshed, to an empty room.

Mark refused to talk to Val when she slunk back to their economy-class cabin but went to eat breakfast with her anyway to escape Kinski, who was now sleeping so heavily that he looked dead. And he really might have been; they were unwilling to investigate. Instead they picked at their pastries in silence, looking out the window at the fast-melting snow, until Kit walked in and sat down with them.

"Shouldn't you be in first class?" Mark asked, glumly.

Val dug through her bag, then handed Kit a cigarette and lighter. "Last ones."

"Salud."

Val put the last remaining cigarette, unlit, in between her lips. "Sorry, Mark. I just had the two left," said Val, with some genuine regret. She really should have thrown a shoe at Kinski or tracked down a porter.

Mark didn't look at her. "Those things are so bad for you."

Kit handed back the lighter, and Val lit her own cigarette. "Well. Part of the appeal."

To Kit, Mark relayed the horrors of the night before. After Val had run off and the madman had, for a moment, wandered out after her, Mark had grabbed his pocketknife and climbed up to hide in Val's top bunk, thinking that higher ground might be safer. Kinski soon returned, and Mark stared at the ceiling until sunrise as the man played solitaire.

"He played *solitaire* in his sleep?"

"He was moving the cards around at any rate. His eyes were sort of opening and closing."

Kit laughed.

"It was unnerving."

"The guy was just really weird. It's hard to describe," Val added. Kit smiled blandly at her. She'd told Mark she spent the night on his floor, and Kit hadn't corrected her.

They were supposed to meet in the first-class dining car for lunch to go over an item as yet unknown with George. Kit had come, ostensibly, to tell them this. Until then, they had time to kill. Without ever consciously agreeing to it, the three of them stayed at their booth until noon—Mark and Val out of uneasiness and Kit out of boredom—ordering coffees occasionally to appease the surly waiter who stalked through the room every twenty minutes.

Mark and Kit spent some time arguing over Jared Diamond, with Mark taking the position that a lack of rigor in his scholarship discredited his ideas and made paleoarchaeology itself look ridiculous, and Kit arguing that while there were flaws in the research, this was inevitable with such a large, complex argument, and at least he was trying to really *say* something. Better to present engaging ideas than to write some massive tome with half its page count taken up by footnotes and an argument irrefutable only because it was too insubstantial to refute. Val doubted that Mark had read the book and knew Kit hadn't. A few days earlier at the airport bookstore, he'd picked it up and carried it around for a while before buying a crime thriller instead, saying that he wanted a distraction from his work and would end up underlining inaccuracies if he bought the Diamond. Both men were rehashing points made in a *New York Times* review of the book that she'd also read. She sipped her coffee in silence.

They'd argued more about principle than exact point. Kit disliked Diamond and didn't bother much with his work, but he also disliked academic criticisms stemming from a fear of anyone trying to say anything at all. As for Mark, Kit had no real issue with him. He was just the sort of person you ended up arguing with. Now Kit felt obligated to smooth things over. As he tried to think up a banal question to demonstrate goodwill, he realized that he knew nothing about Mark's life. Val had said he was a lonely person. And he was American. They could talk about American foreign policy. No. Same problem with the arguing. "How's your thesis going?"

"I haven't started yet."

"Oh." Kit waited for Mark to elaborate and, when he didn't, figured that at least he'd completed his own part in the ritual.

At some point, Val and Kit got up to ask the bartender if he sold cigarettes, and he brought a display case out from under the bar with ten different brands, all in Cyrillic.

"Which is best?" Kit asked.

The bartender shrugged.

Val pointed to a pack near the end that showed a doleful gray dog with a rocket ship behind it and the text "Лайка" below. "It's Laika the space dog," she said.

Kit bent to look. The rocket ship was adorned with a gold hammer and sickle, and the dog, a sharp-eared mutt, seemed to be frowning. He'd read about Laika before, in an unexpectedly brutal illustrated children's book he'd been gifted for his sixth birthday called *Space Race: Make Haste!* The Soviets had caught the dog off the street, named her, trained her, launched her into orbit, and left her to starve alone in the atmosphere. His mother had dug the book out of the garage and presented it to him upon the birth of his son.

"We have no more," said the bartender.

"No Laikas?" Val asked, disappointed.

"The factory close."

Another pack, with a longer and less intelligible name, was decorated with a map of Russia. "These, then," she said, pointing. "For the map."

The bartender smiled. "Belomors? You want these?"

The Russian cigarettes soon proved challenging. Instead of filters, they had cardboard tubes at the end, and Kit swallowed some loose tobacco when he tried to inhale. Val couldn't stop coughing, and both were sick after a few puffs. Kit stubbed his out in the ashtray, but Val suffered through hers. They spent about twenty minutes theorizing about the meeting George was calling.

They'd had half a dozen meetings already to go over scheduling, safety protocols, liability waivers for the university, money exchange rates, and travel tips. And, of course, they'd extensively reviewed the archaeological record of the Northern Yakutia region, and of the Malova Valley specifically, though information here was sparse. Alexey Okladnikov had performed preliminary surveys of the area in the sixties but never followed up. Petroglyphs of uncertain origin had been recorded on the foot of a cliff at a distance of some miles from their cave, and locals sometimes found flint tools in dried riverbeds, but there was nothing else of note. What George had found here that made him come back with students and funding, none of them knew.

Mark wondered if he wanted to change course, to excavate some new area; if the unremarkable Malova basin was actually a decoy.

"He wouldn't do that," Val said. "People always guard their finds."

Mark began to argue, but before he could say much, Val's strange friend appeared in yesterday's button-down, vodka on his breath. Val's fondness for strangers really was unaccountable. She seemed to attract them magnetically; the stranger the stranger, the stronger the pull. And to see her with them, so passive, sometimes ironic but only in the most agreeable way—no sense of self-preservation either—felt almost voyeuristic to Kit. They had taken the same public bus route for the first year of grad school, and on it he'd once witnessed her pretend to believe in astrology for the benefit of a strung-out bald woman with FREE TATOO tattooed onto her arm.

"Lady Di!" said this new lunatic, sitting down in the only empty space in the booth, next to Mark.

"Hi, Doug."

"Hello?" said Mark.

Doug sniffed, vaguely nauseous, then picked the cigarette pack up from the table. "You smoke fucking Belomors? You working construction?"

"What are they?" Val asked. "We just picked them for the packaging."

Doug laughed. "*Picked 'em for the packaging.* Course you did. Okay, so they're sorta like Newports."

"Newports?"

"Yeah."

"We're from Canada," said Mark.

"Canadians, eh? I was in Canada once. Milk in a plastic bag, you freaks. Well, what's the cheapo cig brand up north?"

"Player's," said Val.

"Okay, these are like Player's hit with a blast of nuclear radiation. The guys who built my client's house smoked these things. A group of those guys on break? You couldn't see their faces through the smoke. Belomors are fucking poison, three times as strong as anything you can get in the West. I felt sick just walking past, Christ. These Russians do not fuck around."

Mark laughed with satisfaction.

"Mark," asked Val, "what time is it?"

He looked down at his wrist, found it empty, and said nothing.

"Five o'clock somewhere," said Doug.

Mark soon came up with a bitter pretense of an excuse and found somewhere else to be, though Val wasn't sure where else he could have hidden from their bunkmate. Maybe he really hated her enough that he preferred Klaus Kinski's company to hers.

"So what are you people doing here really?" Doug asked, as soon as they were alone. "CIA? KGB? Don't think for a moment those guys aren't still in the game. But maybe you know that already. Now, you've got nothing to worry about from me—I'm not political. I don't even vote. The world is run behind locked doors, and you can't find your angle until you accept that simple fact." He punctuated this line with a pinching of his yellow fingers.

"We're archaeologists."

Doug took a swig of his coffee. "Oh, okay."

"No, really." She pulled out her JanSport backpack, unzipped it, and presented Doug with her archaeological field pass, tucked into her wallet. Doug turned it over in his hands and returned it. His look was more amused than alarmed, but she understood his point: her spy handlers would provide her with the appropriate forged documents, of course. She pulled out her notebook next, filled with handwritten notes from two Canadian digs that she'd brought more for sentimental purposes than because they'd realistically be useful for comparison. He flipped through it, uninterested but mostly convinced.

This was enough. She had nothing to prove to Doug except that she was not an undercover intelligence agent. This might have even been a fun lie to keep up for the last two days of their journey, but it seemed unwise to let a person so fond of talking go around telling the story of the CIA/KGB spooks posing as a team of Canadian archaeologists whom he'd met on the Trans-Siberian.

"I don't get the draw."

"No?"

He laid his hands out on the table. "You should be sipping champagne in a ballroom, Di"—(the revelation of her true name had made no impression)—"not digging for monkey bones in a melted ice block."

She laughed. "But I never learned ballroom dancing."

"You'd be a natural. Elegant. Like Audrey Hepburn. She was a Canadian, you know."

She was not. "Was she?"

"Oh yeah. That's what made her so exotic, in those days. The guys, well, you probably think you know all about guys, Di, but you don't *really* know guys. The guys like a Marilyn type, blond bombshell." He sculpted an hourglass figure in the air. "But give me an Audrey over a Marilyn any day. No question. Like the choice between black caviar and a Big Mac. You see what I'm saying?" He had at some point begun to sweat visibly, and Val couldn't focus on anything but the beads rolling down his face. One seemed in danger of dropping onto the table.

"Makes sense."

"So, point is, I'd hate to see you ruin your pretty hands clawing through the mud."

"My manicure's not as nice as yours."

He paused, affronted, then looked at his hands, which he'd paused mid-gesture. Seeing his long pinkie nail, he smiled again and shook his head in mock disapproval. "Lady Di, Lady Di. Full of surprises. *My manicure*. Do you part . . . um, partake?"

"Now?"

They both looked around. The bartender nodded gravely at them, and the waiter eyed them peripherally as he took an old man's lunch order. This was stupid.

"One for the road?"

"I couldn't."

"Oh, well."

"I mean, I could . . ."

He fished a baggie out of his sports coat pocket and passed it to her under the table, his sweaty hand lingering for a moment over hers. "Because I like you."

"I won't forget your generosity."

"For when you get bored with your monkey bones."

"I never do."

"I just think," he replied, "that there's something not right about it, digging up buried shit. Kinda nosy. Unnatural. No offense, I mean, I just don't get the draw." He was again gesticulating with unnerving creativity. "And if you wait long enough, you know, it'll all just show up on its own. The world is getting hotter, the ice is melting all by itself. We'll get some mammoths washing up in no time. Hell, why do you think they bothered to build a railroad this far out? It's not easy. The metal freezes. But I'll tell you why they bothered: because it's gonna be the most fertile farmland in the world!"

He talked some more about his plans to irrigate Siberia and the esoteric shifting of the tides of global capital, but Val found herself surprised at how offended she'd felt at his indictment of archaeology. Unnatural. Not right to dig up buried things. *What about fossil fuels?* she might ask him. But then he'd imply that her interests were frivolous in comparison to the demands of the dollar, and she'd have to point out that currency was a social construct with no inherent value, and then they'd argue just after he'd given her free drugs.

The last two days of the trip were uneventful. Val kept to herself and kept busy. They would all see enough of one another in the Malova Valley, so there was no pressing need to socialize. The four of them met up once more in the first-class dining car to talk shop, repeating the same practical details of transportation and geography, the same arguments over Diamond, Okladnikov, carbon dating, and departmental politics. George was as pleasant as ever, but it bothered her now that he wouldn't acknowledge what had happened. Well. Nothing *had* happened. Still, she felt herself retreat into defensive reserve.

As the train pushed farther north, the nights grew shorter and the twilights stretched longer. She became so accustomed to the motions of the train that when she stepped off to stretch her legs, the ground felt too solid, heavy under her feet. Time and space both felt like abstract concepts, folded into the forward motion of the wheels along their set course and seeming to occur only outside the train. She knew she was bored, but only distantly. When they finally reached Yakutsk, the passengers all stumbled out uneasily, as if shaken from a collective trance.

6

THEY STEPPED OFF THE TRAIN AT YAKUTSK STATION, two hundred miles out from the Arctic Circle. Drop an egg from your window in December and it would freeze before it hit the ground. But in July, the Siberian climate was as wet and hot as any tropical swamp. Flowers bloomed yellow, purple, white; tall stalks of grass grew through cracks in the pavement and leaned toward the sun as it moved through the sky; roving gangs of gnats terrorized sweaty men in cutoff jeans. You had to pay attention to realize that the city was designed with the sole purpose of enduring nine months of arctic assault. The streets were broad in the Soviet way and lined with rectangular buildings all built on stilts to protect their foundations from permafrost. Cars were rare, as they needed to be kept in heated garages through the winter or their engines would atrophy. There were no stray dogs. Any escaped pets froze to death before they could establish a population. All this was explained, quite casually, by George's friend Vasiliy Vasilievich Novikov, who met them at the station with an easy smile and an imported German car.

They would stay just one night here, in Vasiliy's home, before a pilot flew them out to the dig site the next morning. Vasiliy kissed George on the cheeks, right, left, and right again, and called him "my old friend!"

"You like her?" he asked George, gesturing toward either his car or the massive black dog taking up all three seats in the back of it. "Such a pain to get her out here."

He helped Val with her bags, smiled warmly, then forgot about her. She, Mark, and Kit all squeezed together in the back of the car with backpacks on their laps and the dog spread across their feet. It looked lethargic. A patch of fur on its flank had been shaved off, a wound freshly sewn up.

"Sorry about that," Vasiliy said, mostly to Kit. "Took her to the vet today."

Kit nodded. "Of course."

"Is she sick?" asked Mark, stroking the dog's back.

"She got cut up when I took her out hunting. Wolves are an issue out here, but my girl fought to kill—only a weak old wolf, alone. Frou Frou dispatched him quickly. She's a Caucasian shepherd. Do you know them? Most deadly dogs in the world. Bred for fighting off bears, and she'd win too." He glanced backward. "Don't touch her. She's not friendly."

Mark withdrew his hand.

Though his face was vague and his body indifferent, Vasiliy had something heroic in his air. He spoke at length, with grand gestures and serene confidence, driving too fast but with precision. Val knew not to bother with him. She felt he would have nothing to say to her, and this proved true. A certain segment of the world's male population always behaved this way. It had to do with her sense of humor, or possibly her manner of speaking, or maybe her hair, or something else she couldn't quite place. She was not, to these men, what a woman should be, and so not quite a woman at all. Instead she was something alien to be avoided cautiously or, as in Vasiliy's case, so jovially that she might as well not have been present.

She couldn't help but resent this. Even Mark she could meet on the grounds of their mutual antipathy. To be ignored so decisively stung. If she were a man, he would have borne her humor with alacrity.

But George wouldn't like her as a man. She couldn't tell whether she would challenge him like Kit did or fawn like Mark, but either way it would be awful. As a woman, she could say almost anything to him and both mean it and not mean it at the same time. People take a man too seriously. They assume he means what he says. It was better this way, really. And besides, if Vasiliy ignored her, his wolf-slaying dog did not. She sat, gigantic and complacent, across Kit's feet and Mark's, to place her head in Val's lap and let her scratch the soft fur behind her ears.

Vasiliy spoke mostly to George, in English so perfect that complimenting him on it would have been an insult. He was not, as Val had assumed, an archaeologist whom George knew professionally. He'd met George on the Trans-Siberian in 1986, headed north for the first time to oversee a diamond mine after having done something in Moscow that would have gotten other men killed or sent to the gulag. But his father sat on the board for Alrosa, the state mining corporation, so he'd been sent north with a salary rather than a sentence. This was no real consolation to Vasiliy. He was a Moscow man. He had taste. He wasn't fit for a life of inspecting machinery and gnawing on reindeer jerky. Or so he'd said to George over drinks when they'd met one fateful afternoon in the dining car.

But how wrong he'd been! He'd thought he was being sent off to his death, but now he knew he'd been dead before. A life without meaning, without integrity. A sordid life. In Yakutia, he went hunting all through the summer. He killed elk, wolves, even a bear once. And he'd taken a wife. She was a Yakut woman—Sakha, as they called themselves—beautiful, quiet, a very good mother. She'd felt some compulsion to teach him her language, and he'd been smitten enough to submit to the lessons. He picked languages up easily, like George. When a person has a knack for languages, this sort of thing seems harmless. But now she was teaching it to little Vasya. Not quite two years old, but still, his own son with his own name babbling this nonsense. His father had wanted a Russian woman for him. Then why send him to Yakutia? The Russian women in Yakutia all wanted to leave. And he was his own man, always had been. But what had George been up to?

It seemed implausible that there might be suburbs in Siberia, but as he talked, Vasiliy drove straight into them. The houses were on stilts or platforms as they were in the city center, cars were scarce, and the gardens, frozen for nine months out of the year, grew either food crops or incidental wildflowers. Otherwise, they might have been passing through a housing development on the outskirts of Toronto.

This kindled a feeling of dread. Toronto in Siberia. But what had she expected? Reindeer spirits dancing through the aurora borealis? Yakutsk was a city, and this was the nineties. She turned her attention back to the car. Kit was looking out the window but hardly seemed to know where he was. He had some stubborn thought in his head, Val could tell. Mark, squeezed awkwardly into the middle seat, was leaning forward and nodding along with the conversation. George and Vasiliy didn't notice him. They were like children, shoved together in the back of the car and forgotten.

Vasiliy's home was large, but he said it would have been larger had a proper villa been feasible to heat. It was painted white, with incongruently baroque accents framing the windows and door. Marie Antoinette's ice-fishing lodge. His wife opened the door for them. She wore a rayon floral dress, her long hair braided, and little Vasya balanced on her hip, pulling at the braid. Vasiliy, Kit, and George took off their shoes in the doorway. Val mimicked them while Mark strode boldly onward into the living room. Vasiliy introduced his wife as Tuskulaana and said she'd prepared a meal for the weary travelers.

The inside of the house had the most baffling decorating scheme Val had ever seen. It had a mix of European antiques; Chinese prints and vases; fur rugs; mounted heads of deer, moose, and bear; cheap modern furniture; and framed watercolor landscapes—the works of Vasiliy's hobbyist grandfather (a prominent party functionary after the purge, George later said) in the years before his death. All of this, mixed together, gave the sense that the couple had chosen half their furnishings from a Nazi stash of looted treasures, the other half from Ikea, then spent any leftover cash at the local taxidermist's. They did not acknowledge any of this as unusual.

Before dinner, they showered. This gave more relief than Val had realized she needed. After separating the locks of her hair from the oily clump into which they had congealed and washing the dull grime from her face, she felt lighter, energized, and strangely open to the world with the barrier of dirt scrubbed away.

The meal had been arranged in an elaborate spread on a long pine table: fish soup, potatoes, and a meat dish that Mark identified as venison. They ate in that hurried, obliging way that people often eat in unfamiliar homes. Once George had explained where his cave was and declined Vasiliy's offer to lend Frou Frou as protection, there was a lull in the conversation. Vasiliy and George didn't really seem to know each other as well as Val had expected. She felt compelled to say something and so said, "George told us the Malova Valley is haunted."

This earned a general laugh, more to keep up the mood of the room than because what she'd said was especially funny. Val expected it and wasn't much offended.

"I was only repeating an old story I'd been told," said George.

"But is it?" Kit asked Vasiliy.

Vasiliy weighed the question. His wife, who had been silent since introducing herself and looked up only upon hearing the word "Malova," said something to him in a language that must have been Sakha. Vasiliy replied in Russian, and they debated for a minute.

"Not haunted," said Vasiliy, turning back to the table, "but . . . occupied."

Nobody laughed.

"Yes," said Tuskulaana.

Kit set down his fork. "Occupied by whom?"

"It's just a story," Vasiliy explained. "I didn't know. My wife is from a village. She has all these stories. She says that certain parts of Malova are dangerous, are, I don't know, not allowed. Taboo."

Kit picked up his fork again.

"Abrupt atmospheric pressure changes, I'd say. Humans are remarkable at picking them up," said Mark. "And this is great fish soup."

Val ended up in the kitchen with Tuskulaana, drying dishes as they were passed to her. The men remained in the dining room to yell at each other about the American president. Vasiliy mentioned a headline from a newspaper that Mark decried as misleading, and so the homosocial bonding ritual began. Even Kit was drawn into it by the sheer wrongness of an opinion George expressed.

Val had considered obstinately staying behind with them and contributing her own opinion, but the men were loud and drunk. Vasiliy had broken out his best vodka for the guests. And besides, it seemed callous to leave Tuskulaana to bustle about silently like a servant in her own home. The two women communicated occasionally in Russian, but Val spoke it so poorly that they mostly just pointed when necessary. Her host was efficient with the washing, and Val, with the drying.

"You're quick," Tuskulaana commented. Her voice was deeper in Russian than in her own tongue.

Val smiled.

"But in America," she continued, "you have a machine to wash dishes?"

"Some people." It seemed pointless to assert her Canadian identity here.

Tuskulaana spoke again, more quickly, something about American women that Val didn't fully process and a question afterward that she didn't catch a word of. She repeated her question more slowly and with simpler syntax, making steady eye contact. Her face, Val realized, was a very young face. She couldn't have been older than twenty-two or twenty-three. What Tuskulaana wanted to know was "Are you his wife?"

"Oh!" said Val, then in English: "No. Who did you mean? But no. Nyet."

They spoke very little after that and disbanded as soon as their task was finished, with Tuskulaana leading Val past the political debate and into a small storage room where a cot had been set up for her. After brushing her teeth in a half bathroom across the hall, she lay in the half dark for a while, listening to the voices of the men coming loudly, then softly, then loudly again through the walls. She closed her eyes and tried to slow her breathing. Her sister, Lily, had told her once that she was temperamentally nervous because she couldn't breathe properly. She inhaled too shallowly and exhaled too quickly. Lily showed her some meditation breathing exercise, then put her hand on Val's stomach as she practiced, insisting she was doing it wrong. *Breathing* wrong? Yes.

"Well," Val said, "if I can't even breathe right, then just shoot me, just cull me like a deformed farm animal," and Lily told her that if she were breathing right, she wouldn't be so reactive. But really, if she couldn't even breathe, there must be no limit to what she couldn't do. This was a new frontier of incompetence, a feat of devolution. The dining room debate turned to Yeltsin. She got up and walked out through the back door with a pack of Sobranie cigarettes she'd bought on the train.

The house faced a field of many-colored wildflowers, frantic with life. Though it was probably just a plane of frozen dirt for most of the year, this fate seemed remote. Val's shower, stripping a film of oil from her face, had seemed to strip away a layer separating her from the world. Her blood moved through her body with the same steady chirp of the crickets. Her lavender-papered cigarette matched the sky. She felt herself tethered to the earth as she watched its smoke float away. At eleven p.m., the sun was just beginning to really set and would be up again in four hours. Frou Frou, chained to a pole, slept near her, though her ears perked up before Val heard the door creak open. She turned to see George. He smiled very warmly but didn't greet her.

Val had to supply the first: "Hi."

"You have a mosquito here," said George, cupping the side of his own neck.

Val quickly copied his motion and felt the insect die under the pressure of her hand. After inspecting the carnage, she wiped the mangled mosquito corpse and her own siphoned blood discreetly on the underside of the railing, leaving her hand in place as if she were just steadying herself, then offered George a cigarette with her left hand. She was something close to ambidextrous and liked to show it off sometimes. To Val, the Sobranies seemed almost too lovely to smoke. Each was wrapped in a different pastel paper and tipped in gold. George twirled her gift, bubblegum pink, between his thumb and forefinger with more amusement than reverence.

"Did we drive you away?" he asked, sitting down on the steps. She sat down too, so as not to tower over him.

"I thought somebody should help Tuskulaana."

George took a second to process this. Val wasn't sure if he was drunk. He didn't look drunk, but then he would be the type never to show it, self-possession being so deeply ingrained in him that it would simply carry itself forward automatically if inebriation prevented him from presenting it consciously. Or maybe he just hadn't bothered to learn the name of his hostess.

"Vasiliy's wife," Val clarified.

"Ah."

She handed him her lighter.

"You could come back," he offered. "Vasiliy doesn't care if you smoke inside."

"Sadly I don't have much to contribute on the topic of Yeltsin's trade relations."

"Neither do they."

"But they're louder."

He laughed. "Vasiliy thought you were upset. He sent me to check on you."

"Upset?" She was surprised both at the idea that Vasiliy was concerned and at the cause of concern. *Was* she upset?

"I told him you were fine."

"I'm just glad that we'll finally be getting to work."

"Val," said George.

Usually she didn't like to be addressed by name. It felt too intimate, an intrusion, a maneuver. Her father had told her that people love to hear their own names, and she'd heard once that they taught students in business school to use them as much as possible during negotiations. Now whenever someone began a sentence with "Val" or, God forbid, "Valerie," she wondered what they wanted from her and how she could stop them from getting it. But with George it was just natural. Everything he did seemed exactly what it should be, even when it surprised her.

"Sometimes I worry that you don't have the most pragmatic approach to the world."

Val heard herself laugh. "What does that even mean?"

"You take things too personally. Don't embrace the grander view," he said, without accusation.

"Well. You've got me wrong. The grander view is—It's the whole point of things, right? It's what's so brilliant about the work. Connecting, through time and space, what makes us . . ." A brown rabbit loped through the wildflowers with nervous elegance. She had meant to say *what makes us human* but had become suddenly self-conscious. "It's just all very . . ." She waved her left hand in a vague way, right hand still clutching the rail. "I have the right approach to the work, anyway."

George nodded. They both looked straight ahead at the rabbit.

"How do those survive here through the winter?" Val asked, pointing with her cigarette.

"They grow thick coats. They turn white."

Val laughed. There was something lovely about that idea. "I guess we turn darker in the summer too."

Saying nothing, George's hand came down on her shoulder with a clap. "You had another mosquito," he said.

Val brought her hand protectively over the place where his had just been and peeled off the corpse of the bug. "They love me."

"It's probably your blood type."

"Really?"

"They're most attracted to type O."

"I don't know mine. Is that bad?"

"They always test before giving a transfusion, and if not they just give you O negative, the universal donor."

He told her about a woman he'd known who needed a blood transfusion after a car accident. Based on her blood type, she learned she'd been the product of an affair. "Actually," he added, "she was my wife."

Val remembered this wife. She used to see them walking together on campus. He, a star in his field, hair and eyes as black as tar, tall and well-built in his tailored suits, strolling with the ease that only those born into money could ever achieve; she, adjunct French professor, striding to keep up on her little legs, face beaky, body hunched and small, always in some oppressive brown skirt set. But people chose each other for all sorts of reasons. These sightings were all in the early days of Val's undergrad career. She had at some point stopped seeing them together, although she couldn't say when exactly. He would talk happily and at length about losing a pinkie toe to frostbite or even of a youthful dalliance in Mongolia some fifteen years back that ended with a romantic rival attempting to contract an Altai shaman to curse him, but he never mentioned his marriage. She knew only that he lived alone now.

"Did she . . . in the accident, I mean . . ."

"Did she die? No, but it seemed to spark an existential crisis. Now she has a tenure track position in Alberta."

Val laughed, a little spiteful. "Is there a difference?"

"Edmonton is pretty in the springtime."

She kept her eyes on a pair of white butterflies chasing each other through the flowers but could hear the amusement in his voice. He had such a way, sometimes, of making her feel as if the whole world were a joke, and they were the only ones in on it. The butterflies dove down below the flowers and disappeared.

"Tuskulaana thought *I* was your wife."

"Did she?"

Val had expected him to laugh, but his voice was low, the inflection slight. She turned to look at him. His hair, still damp from his shower and free from its usual product, fell dark and disordered over his forehead; his skin, scrubbed fresh, was just beginning to form a dew of sweat from the humid twilight. His eyes met hers. Usually she had to look up to see his face, but sitting beside him on the steps, it was almost level with her own. She knew she could have him if she wanted him.

She'd thought about it before, more than once. He was handsome, worldly, so self-assured as to seem almost mythical when she thought of him. And she'd seen him look at her in that way. At dinner, in Moscow, he'd done it. And on the train, when she'd slept in his unmade bed, smelled his shampoo on the pillow. Sometimes she even felt that she loved him, for what he'd given her. She couldn't bear to hear him criticized. And now she could have him, and part of her thought less of him for it, for lowering himself to the level of man, an animal. He was supposed to be a myth.

She drew her Sobranie to her lips and found only a long finger of ash remained, pointing at him, accusing, beckoning. A breeze blew the ash away, and she kissed him.

7

"Archaeology, man! Indiana Jones!" Anatoliy said to nobody in particular. He was at that moment flying a twelve-seat An-2 crop-dusting plane over an expanse of Siberian tundra, conveying George, Val, Kit, and Mark to their destination in the Malova Valley.

His passengers sat in silent horror. As absurd as the concept of an Egyptian temple built to house an Israelite artifact was, Val, Kit, and Mark had all felt real pain as teenagers, watching Harrison Ford swing from its ceilings and knock it to dust. None of them bought tickets to the sequels. In academic archaeology, "Indiana Jones" was used occasionally as a slur, such as when the head of the department said of George's biplane aerial survey, "Look at you! Indiana Jones." Some of the older professors at the university would often claim they planned to retire in five years, when the eldest of the *Indiana Jones* generation reached adulthood and began to apply to graduate school.

"I love American movies. I see them all, learn my English from them. You Americans, great movies."

"We're actually Canadian," said Mark, who was in fact an American. He'd told Val, on their single horrible date, that he grew up on a trout farm outside Juneau, Alaska.

"But you watch Spielberg, yes?"

"Yes," said Val.

"He is genius, like the Andrey Sakharov of movies. Soviets did great science movies? Not so much my style. But your Spielberg I love. *Jaws*, wow. What else? E.T. phone home! A great film as well, I think, although perhaps a bit for child? What is the word?"

"'Childish.'"

"Yes, childish. But still I like. And you know what else? George Lucas, *Star Wars*."

"*Star Wars* is an excellent franchise," Mark agreed.

"The little Ewok I love. Like bear cub, fierce."

"Did you think the Ewoks were . . . a tonally appropriate inclusion?"

This went on for some time. Kit said nothing, genuinely frightened by the small plane and its pilot's cavalier attitude. Val peered out the window so as not to look anywhere else. They were above the mountains now.

"Ma*jesty*," said Anatoliy, gesturing outward with a hand he should have been steering with, but these were sloping little things. Kit let out an involuntary yelp. He was clutching the edge of his seat and staring at his knees. Val studied the mountains. They must have met some official height requirement to be termed mountains, because everyone called them the Malova Mountains, but from above they looked like hills. She was reminded of the old theory that Earth's magma core was cooling and contracting, causing Earth to shrink and making mountain ranges out of wrinkled excess crust. Earth, they knew now, was actually getting warmer, and while this brought its own dread, it did seem better than a desolate, shrunken ice rock of a planet, covered in pug-faced mountains.

"*Inside Majesty's Secret Service*," said Anatoliy. "Not best James Bond. I have seen them all."

George laughed at this, and everybody looked at him, surprised. He'd been silent and abstracted all morning. Val had been trying not to meet his eye, a feat in a half-full twelve-seat plane, but she did now, and it burned. Of course Earth was getting warmer. How could anyone have believed otherwise? She watched him turn back to Anatoliy, now amiable, and ask if he'd been in the air force and to tell him all about it. She hadn't spoken to him alone since the previous evening. After they'd kissed, they talked for another hour, the kiss lingering but unacknowledged, and then they'd kissed again, and he'd said, "It would be wise, you know, to keep this between ourselves."

Now that she'd had a taste, she wanted him fully. To feel him touch her, to take him inside her, to have his body wrapped around hers, to dissolve into him. She was mortified by the sudden, adolescent intensity of this need, but mortification did nothing to cool it. Before, everything had been hypothetical. She could laugh about George—try to get Kit to admit that he had nice arms, defend him rather carelessly against claims of arrogance (calling arrogance a virtue rather than denying that George possessed the quality), and juggle any number of people in her head as attractive or interesting. He had been comfortable because he'd been off-limits.

But she'd trespassed those limits. An impulse of the moment. She just as easily could have cracked a joke, changed the subject. But now that it was done, it seemed inevitable. Maybe she'd known all along she would do it. Her eyes closed of their own volition.

It was still midmorning. They'd left early, not out of any urgent necessity but because all of them happened to be awake and George, anxious to begin, had called Anatoliy and asked him to meet them two hours earlier than they'd planned. They rode in silence to the airstrip, which was really just a slab of asphalt littered with undersized hand-me-down aircrafts in varying states of decay. Vasiliy left them with a simple "Good luck, my friends!" and they were off.

Val hadn't slept at all the night before. She'd sat out alone for a while after he left her and smoked a yellow Sobranie before it grew dark. Her legs were devoured by mosquitoes, and later she regretted this carelessness, but it had seemed impossible to go back into the house. The thought that she might see him again paralyzed her. Who knew what he was thinking? He could be realizing that she was actually a rather annoying person, with unoriginal ideas and a sentimental worldview. It was unbearable. He shouldn't be allowed to think anything about her at all, even good things. The rabbit returned to nibble on some weeds, and Frou Frou suddenly lunged for it. She had it between her jaws before Val understood what was happening and began to shake. The rabbit let out a loud, high shriek, a sound Val didn't know rabbits could make, and was dead within a minute. Val, for a moment, thought she might cry. Maybe it was a different rabbit, she reasoned, as if that somehow made things better. She knew what George would say. Or Mark, or Kit, or anybody really. Circle of life, natural balance, population control, ecosystems. Frou Frou, coated in fresh blood, wagged her tail and began to decapitate the corpse, holding the body with her front paws and pulling at the skull with her teeth. Only then did Val go inside, quietly and without turning on any lights.

As much as she wanted to avoid George, she didn't want to see the others either. They'd know somehow, just by looking at her. Having been raised without religion, she wasn't squeamish about sex. And this had only been a kiss. She was being ridiculous. Immature. She wanted him. She wished she'd never met him. This terrible combination of desires kept her up all night like an instrument of the inquisition designed to make its victims agonizingly aware at all times of their bodies. And even now, she'd be forced back into wakefulness whenever she felt herself drift off, either by a jolt of memory or by the lurching of the plane as Anatoliy veered sideways to point out some feature of the geography to George.

They were dropped in a clearing below the foothills of the Malova Mountains around noon, according to Kit. Mark still had no watch and had to rely on this vague report. Anatoliy helped unload a few crates of supplies, quoted the Terminator, and flew off, leaving them to take in the silence.

At a distance of a few hundred feet, a limestone cliffside loomed over them, casting a shadow over the clearing. George pointed up in the direction of the cave, which he said sat midway up the closest hill, tucked against the cliff. A natural path could be seen at a distance through the white rocks, steep but walkable.

On the other side of the clearing, a pine forest started up rather abruptly. The Malova River was close by. Mark could hear it through the trees but couldn't see it. The sky was still blue. It would turn purple late into the night, then remain that way until two in the morning.

"Well," said Valerie.

George clapped his hands together and said they'd better start building.

They constructed their tents, three red nylon structures with slack inner layers of mosquito netting, along with a battered reindeer-hide yurt George had used for each expedition since his first foray into the Siberian tundra. After this, Mark set up the gas stove and gathered rocks for a firepit, while Val unpacked and organized their tools in a collapsible deck box. For half the afternoon, Kit and George were occupied with attempts to set up the satellite phone— a finicky brick weighing thirty pounds accompanied by a slim, incomprehensible instructions booklet—under a canopy at the center of the camp. Mark cooked up a lunch of beans and fried toast, which everybody ate with relish. A certain anxious camaraderie had sprung up among them. There couldn't be another human being around for fifty miles in any direction.

Work was completed by five. They had decided to hike up to the cave the next morning, but this left a restless, empty evening to fill. Mark wasn't tired in the slightest and had to stop himself from going up to the cave on his own, just to look around. It wasn't sportsmanlike, and George would disapprove. Instead, he took out *STALIN* to stare at and parked himself on one of the camping chairs he'd placed around the stove.

"Ah," said George, who had managed to creep up behind him. "That's an excellent book. Impeccably researched." He gave him an encouraging smile, then left to refill his water bottle. Mark felt flattered by George's approval until he realized this meant he'd actually have to read *STALIN*.

Val prepared a mediocre canned dinner, and they sat around the fire together, sweating, swatting away mosquitoes, and talking with more energy than they'd summoned since first arriving in Russia.

"This reminds me," said Val, "of camping as a kid. We could tell ghost stories."

"I never went camping as a kid. There's something contrived about the whole practice," replied Kit.

"I never went either. I just mean it reminds me of what it probably feels like to be a child, camping."

"Why not like an adult camping?" said Mark. "I mean, we *are* camping. And we're adults."

"But it doesn't count as camping if you're doing it for a reason. Camping is supposed to be pointlessly uncomfortable. And then you have some profound revelation or at least feel like a good person for having gone camping."

"It counts. I don't see how it wouldn't *count*—"

"But no, I see what you mean," said Kit. "It's this mimicry, this sort of gesture toward a past where people underwent deprivation as a necessity, only now it's somehow supposed to be fun."

Val and Mark both insisted that he was failing to grasp the charm of camping, but this uneasy alliance fell apart when Val, now sincere, defined it as a feeling of wonder at the scale and complexity and mystery of the world around us, and Mark contended that it was really a test of one's self-sufficiency. "Besides," he couldn't help but add, "you just admitted that you'd never been camping."

"Let's use your definition and say we're camping now."

George, who had been going over some account book with his fountain pen—an absurd, miraculous object to be holding so casually in the depths of the Siberian tundra—looked up and smiled slightly. Though he contributed little materially, there was an extent to which this conversation was held for his benefit. Without realizing it, they gave extra context to their arguments and chose their words more carefully. Even Kit, on some level, needed George to know he was smart. Mark was no better.

They sat around talking for a while after they'd finished eating and eventually lapsed into silence.

"What time is it?" Mark asked eventually.

"Eight," said Kit. "It won't get dark for six hours."

Nobody replied. Valerie opened her backpack, riffling through until she pulled out a pack of cigarettes.

"It might not hurt to walk up to the cave," said Mark, "just so we know what we're dealing with tomorrow."

They all looked at George, who thought for a second, nodded, and stood up. Once he was above them, he smiled obligingly. Val put away her unsmoked cigarette, Kit laced up his stiff new boots, and they left.

Archaeology considered itself a science, but in truth, most of its practitioners were romantic types. Though their field demanded scientific precision and rigor, they hailed from backgrounds in history, art, and literature and, as such, had aspirations as poetic as they were scientific. Though embarrassed to admit it, they wanted to unlock the key to human nature. This meant that Kit was highly valued for his ability to do basic math in his head, to balance chemical equations, and to convert basic measurements without the aid of a calculator. He was writing his thesis on the effects geologic conditions wrought upon human habitation patterns and generally brought an air of seriousness to the endeavor.

George had told him he'd brought him along for his knowledge of geology—said he thought it would be helpful to have somebody else to consult who actually knew what he was talking about. This had seemed to be a rather transparent manipulation at the time, but now, as he saw Mark and Val look around the cave with awe, imbuing each rock with some sort of ancient, esoteric knowledge, he realized there was some truth in it too.

First, one had to look at the facts.

George had pointed out some smooth, even pits in the ground right before the cave's opening: grinding basins to crush seeds and minerals, a telltale sign of long-term habitation. After climbing through the sharp racks at its entrance, the cave was about as tall as it was wide, spacious, and easy to walk through, making it an ideal shelter, with the passage only narrowing after the light faded.

Human beings never lived in caves permanently and in large numbers. This was a common misconception. People needed light to live and open air. And a fire could not be lit in a cave with a single opening without suffocating all its inhabitants. Instead, caves were temporary shelters during journeys and long hunts. Nomadic people would set up their camps at the mouths of caves then move on after a period of days, weeks, months, depending on the weather, the migration patterns of antelope or reindeer, luck. And this transient use would often continue for tens of thousands of years.

In colder climates like this, people sometimes stayed in caves for longer periods during the winter. The temperature of a cave, mediated by the soil and rock surrounding it, didn't vary so much as the temperature of the air outside it. Now, in the summer, cool air emanated from the cave, wet but not unclean. Light penetrated about fifty feet past the mouth before its consummation in darkness. Its air was cool. And when they'd stepped in, they all felt something—something very old but immediate. This was the closest thing Kit knew to religion, this feeling of the past reaching out to touch him. It was the best part of his work. Val had said, after their dinner in Moscow, that she was surprised by how much stock he put in superstition and ghost stories. This disconnect arose, probably, because he could do math, and because he could control his face, could keep it from falling slack with romantic awe.

It was something deeply instinctual to regard a cave as holy. Consistently through time and across the world, caves were used as ritual sites. And curiously, most examples were found in the caves' dark zones, where no light penetrated. In Altamira and Lascaux, caves had been found covered in paintings. Animals running across the walls: herds of bison, wild horses overlapping, sometimes a boar or mammoth. Handprints in relief, applied in clusters over millennia, one sometimes two thousand years older than another applied right beside it. In the Americas, the practice of cave painting persisted longer. The Cherokee would write backward in caves, so spirits on the other side of the rock could read their messages. This cave seemed like a place to send messages to spirits, and maybe to hear back, but Kit would never think to say a thing like that out loud. He put his hand up to the cold rock, feeling its solidity. All around him, the world seemed to coalesce into a deep hum.

Mark was kept up by thoughts of the cave. Closing his eyes, he'd find himself walking through it again, seeing its contours, feeling the cool air move through it. He had assumed he'd sleep better than the others, having been raised in a place with long summer twilights. It reminded him of June in Alaska, when nights wouldn't even last five hours. Growing up, he'd worked on the farm during summer holidays and spent his free hours reading or walking aimlessly. Talking to nobody for months except at Scout troop meetings, wandering through the woods until the sun set at one in the morning, reading Lovecraft in the pines, burning, freckling, bathing rarely, he would grow over the course of each summer to think he was entirely unlike other people. A separate species, almost.

An interruption cutting through the light startled him from his thoughts. Even at its darkest hour, night had never fully overtook the farm at the height of summer, and it was the same here. He could clearly see a shadow passing his tent. A small figure, taking small steps. She couldn't be stupid enough to be taking a walk now. George had impressed upon them the dangers of the taiga, even with precautions taken. But maybe she needed something from George. They were always off in a corner, talking. She'd spend ninety minutes with him during office hours while Mark sat around outside, and George was always too polite to tell her to leave.

But it wasn't just politeness. He sometimes felt that, though his conversations with George were more complex and substantial, he preferred talking to her. She was often vague on facts, unscientific, unserious, but she could make him laugh when Mark never could. He could only see her now as a shadow staining the bright screen of his tent, and then she was gone.

And she was so slight, like a fairy or a child. It must be nice, in a way, to be small, to not constantly have to apologize for moving through a world not built to accommodate you. He didn't *mean* to take up so much space, but he was fated to be tall and broad, and notably so. To be notably big in a world where bigness gave no advantage made him faintly ridiculous, like a man wearing hiking boots for a walk in the park. In the university's older buildings, he had to duck and squeeze through doors. Swivel chairs dipped under his weight. As Valerie had once told him, "It looks like you're an adult trying to fit into a child's playhouse." On that occasion, she'd actually been trying to be friendly. Still, there was always an edge.

But no more Valerie Howe. He knew he must spend more time thinking about her than she did about him, and this felt both unfair and undignified. What had he been thinking about before? Alaska. How stupid it was to think you were different from other people.

Mark woke early and took a walk, feeling not at all like himself. Or, rather, he felt like a past version of himself, from adolescence, and was discomfited by the idea that this old self (whom he would have thought dead if he'd thought about it at all) could so easily possess him again. It was the sky that did it. The sky and the trees. He walked down to the river, intending to trace its bank so as not to lose his way in the forest. There were no trails here and no people to make them. It didn't feel lonely, exactly. A concept like loneliness was too human to apply.

As soon as he reached the river, though, he saw a figure standing near the edge. Smoking a cigarette, paperback tucked under her arm. She didn't see him, and at first, he didn't want her to see him. He thought of turning back, but it seemed even worse to risk her noticing his presence only as he slunk away, so he shuffled and dragged his footsteps through the pine needles to alert her without any interaction needed. Still, she didn't move, except to ash the cigarette. He resorted to clearing his throat, and she turned her head instantly, making a small sound of alarm before regaining composure.

"How are you?" Valerie asked.

"Good."

"That's good." She could be like this sometimes, speaking so tritely, with no hint of self-consciousness, that she seemed slightly stupid.

"I could see you from back there." Mark gestured backward with his chin.

She laughed. "You just brought up the strangest memory."

She paused. He did not reply, but stood awkwardly a few feet away.

"My mother, when I was really little, she had this blue silk fan, gold on the edges with birds, or a dragon? Anyways, she held it up in front of her face and said, 'I can see you, but you can't see me.'"

"That's . . . what's the word?"

"'Evocative'?" She was looking past him, at the low sun to the east.

"No, it'll come to me."

"The fan is still somewhere in my father's house. Nobody cared about it. It's just one of those things you can't throw out because it's been around so long, so you push it around into different drawers in spring cleaning. Maybe that's why I retained the memory. I used to imagine her in Heaven looking down on me and saying it again, you know: 'I can see you, but you can't see me.'"

"Maybe she is," Mark offered.

"She's not."

He thought of his own mother, large and red-haired like himself, serving Hamburger Helper, quoting the Gospel from memory. She had tried to protect him, but from the wrong things. Now he called on holidays, and to her credit, she always did seem pleased to hear his voice. "How did she die?"

Val took a drag of her cigarette. "Lung cancer."

"Lung cancer?"

She shrugged, daring him to elaborate. And he could have elaborated, at length, if he had been himself that morning.

"I remembered the word."

"Yeah?"

"'Disquieting.'"

"*Disquieting.* Well, now that you say it, I never realized how creepy it is." She laughed again, staring at the rocks below the river. Her arms were bare, marked up with bug bites and a few freckles floating at the tops of her sharp shoulders.

"What are you reading?"

She held up the book so he could read the title—the same one she'd been reading on the train—then tucked it back under her arm. The mood had shifted suddenly, and this small gesture of contempt punctured sharply, inoculating him against all sentiment. He nodded at her and walked on.

Once moving again, he realized he'd felt her snub too keenly. Perhaps he'd read too much into it. She wasn't so bad, really. Just a bit obvious. The short hair. The cigarettes. *Howards End.* The dead mother. She was a person who relied on appearances—not an uncommon fault. Maybe he'd be the same if he had the luxury, but it was easier for girls.

A sound from the forest startled him out of uncharitable thoughts. In the Boy Scouts, he'd learned about the sounds of the forest. This was a living creature, and not a small one either. The noise stilled, as if whatever had made it heard him too. There were bears in these woods, and wolves. Were they too far north for Siberian tigers? He took a step forward, willing himself not to show fear. Your best chance against a bear was to stand rooted in place, make yourself as large as possible, shout, and wave your arms. They were territorial but capricious animals who might just as well saunter off as rip your ribs apart. Wolves hunted in packs and only for food. A lone wolf, he might scare off. A hungry pack would certainly kill him. But this creature, emerging from the trees, was neither bear nor wolf. It was George.

"You're up early!" he said cheerfully. There was something burning in his eyes that he was doing his best to extinguish with good humor. His passion, Mark thought, was his most admirable quality, but he was too composed to display it very often.

"I was doing a bit of scouting," Mark explained, almost apologetic.

"Why not wait for the undergrads?"

Mark knew reconnaissance was tedious work, involving teams of young people walking out a hundred yards in all directions from a single point, counting pottery sherds in the topsoil as they went to identify areas of high activity. He had done it as an undergrad on a dig in Israel and had taken the task very seriously at the time. The director of the project had stressed the importance of walking in a perfectly straight line, even if that meant soaking your steel-toed boots in a creek or sliding down a small cliff. Though a flag was placed to mark his destination, he'd started his first reconnaissance walk holding a compass in front of him, to make sure he didn't deviate a degree from his assigned direction. They sent him through a field overgrown with brambles, and he ended the walk with his khakis torn to shreds, his legs cut up and bloody under the uneven start of a sunburn.

This, of course, had been on the outskirts of a small, well-worn site first settled in the neolithic. He had no idea how much more frustrating and arbitrary the practice would prove to be in the Siberian taiga, sparse in artifacts, dense in trees and apex predators, and where there was no pottery in the topsoil and walking in a perfectly straight line for a hundred yards would incur a hundred concussions and perhaps a mauling. The undergrads might just as well be left out of the equation.

George, with perfect manners, didn't raise any of these objections. "Of course once the site is established," he said, "we'll conduct more thorough searches. But I happened to wake up early, like you."

"Valerie's up too."

"Did you remember your bear spray?"

He admitted he had not.

"Always keep it on your person."

Mark nodded and wondered if he should mention he'd been an Eagle Scout. George probably remembered.

"I don't bother with it myself, of course," George continued. "I survived the eighties without it, but it wouldn't look very good if I let my students get eaten."

"Makes sense."

He worried, suddenly, about Valerie all alone by the river and then felt stupid again.

8

Val had seen him hammer each wooden pole into the ground, attach the hide covering, and drag each light item of furniture in: a bamboo foldout desk and chair, an old Persian rug to hide the tarp floor, the Olivetti in its battered black case, some sort of padded cotton sleeping mat, which rolled out to the size of a double bed. He had taken nothing superfluous—no crystal decanter, no heavy cotton paper. He'd packed necessary objects only, and yet they seemed too luxurious, too personal, too old. The deer-hide covering, at least, had to be overkill. Val, Kit, and Mark had brought hideous plastic camping gear purchased begrudgingly at exorbitant expense—this felt more professional. George didn't need to feel professional. Taken individually, his objects had seemed a little ridiculous, but set together in the light of his gas lamp, under the unifying force of his personality, the effect was shockingly civilized, undeniably correct.

She had come in the first hour of darkness; there would be only three. She knew he would be awake, and he was. She needed to see him. He let her in, and she sat uninvited on the edge of his bed mat. He sat too.

"I think . . ." she said. And then nothing more. He moved a lock of hair from her forehead. Her hair was a little too short for this act to feel entirely natural. Perhaps this was what he always did, tenderly rearrange a single lock of hair. *In order to see your face better, to really see you.* But the important thing was not to think. She didn't finish her sentence. She didn't think. She touched his face, right under the jaw. He hadn't shaved that day, and she liked the roughness of his skin, the way it felt so unlike her own. She took the top button of his shirt in her hand. It was mother-of-pearl, with the dull side turned out to face the world, bright abalone set inward against the fabric. An edge of oil-slick rainbow flashed in the gaslight as she pulled it free of its buttonhole. How luxurious, to buy rainbow shell buttons sewn in as secrets. He unbuttoned the rest on his own.

Val knew she was a bad lover, generally, but men never seemed to notice. The problem was that she couldn't relax. She was always directing herself: *And now I put my leg like this. And now I arch my back. And now I make this face. And, oh God, not that face. And what sort of face is it that he's making? Does he know he looks like that?*

She'd experimented with drunk sex. High sex. Sex on cocaine. But this sort of thing always made her queasy; it drew out the panting, squelching, repulsive aspects of the act, and she wouldn't even want to shake hands with another person for weeks afterward. And the point wasn't just to endure it. The point was to be close or satisfied, or to remember you're an entire animal and not just some floating, chattering head. Well. Why did anybody do anything?

It was true that she'd felt moments of connection, but in general, she was a bad lover, and most other people were bad lovers too, focused on the ritual rather than its meaning. And the good lovers were never the ones you expected or the ones you wanted. They weren't the kindest or the most honest people. Just those who had the ability to leave themselves. Maybe it was easier in the past, when narratives around sex were less baroque. But maybe not.

When they'd finished, some men would stretch an arm out around her shoulders and sigh with satisfaction. Others would ask, plaintively, "Was that good for you?" George took out two cigarettes, handed one to her, and lit it as it balanced between her lips with an engraved silver lighter. The flame burned her retinas for a moment, then died. They ashed into a tin coffee cup set between them. He didn't seem to want to talk, and that suited her. She felt comfortably blank. The point of sex, she thought, must be to smoke a cigarette afterward.

And then a shot of panic. She was in his tent. She'd snuck in under the cover of night, at the darkest hour when she was sure she couldn't be seen; whispered through the fabric to ask if he was awake, said she needed to talk, and realized she hadn't even thought of a pretense. What sort of person behaved like this? This was sordid. She sat up.

"It's all right," he said now, reading her face.

"I just wish we had more privacy."

"Nobody's going to pry. We're all adults."

"Adults who chose a career centered around prying."

Half propped up on his elbow like a Roman emperor in repose, he smiled, took a drag.

"I just wish things were clearer." This sounded banal and vague even for melancholy pillow talk, but she didn't quite know how to say what she meant.

George thought about it for a few seconds. "Things do get clearer."

Val felt that he didn't fully understand her meaning, or perhaps that he was naturally a very specific and cohesive person, so had never had occasion to wonder about it.

You'll understand when you're older—that was the tenor his answer took. Maybe she should be offended by this. She was twenty-five with a promising career ahead if she kept it all together. But she wasn't offended. She put her head on his chest and closed her eyes. She breathed in the scent of his skin, felt the warmth of his blood underneath, heard the steady beat of his heart pushing upward in even intervals to meet her cheek. His hand traced a lazy circle on her shoulder. It was reassuring to be around somebody with an ordered mind, somebody for whom things made sense. She wanted to tell him to explain how the world worked. Or, if that was too much, to at least reassure her that it *was* somehow working. "I hope so," she said.

When Kit woke at seven, they gathered for a granola breakfast and left quickly for the cave. They wanted to get some pre-excavation work done before the heat really set in. By midday, it would get so hot at the mouth of the cave that dehydration headaches were inevitable, no matter how much water they drank. Val took photographs of the mouth, entrance zone, and twilight zone, while Kit sketched its geologic features. Mark and George stood around tapping their feet and talking about nothing until they could begin to set up a grid along the floor of the cave, hammering down a wooden stake every square meter. Mark kept tripping over the stakes, but everybody pretended not to notice. Though they could have waited until the next day to do it, they started to dig out test pits in the late afternoon. Initially, two were to be excavated in each zone of the cave—the mouth, the entrance zone, and the twilight zone—excluding the long, imposing dark zone. George felt they shouldn't bother with it on this trip. Dark zones were difficult to navigate, requiring bright lights with heavy batteries to excavate, and as they were not practical living spaces, artifacts were rare. This cave was unexplored too, and possibly dangerous.

By lunch the next day, the test pits in the mouth of the cave were half done, and they'd found nothing but animal bones, though one of these had what might have been knife marks on them. That is, Kit thought the notches came from a stone knife and Val agreed, but Mark said they were probably just from the claws of an ancient cave bear or even a modern bear, and George, with less interest than his students had expected, said they'd send it off for analysis at the end of the summer.

That afternoon, as they hunched over their test pits, straightening the baulks, a cool wind blew across the tops of their backs from inside the cave. Val looked to George, who said, "Just a shift in pressure," while looking at Kit, who in fact knew more about the workings of geology than anybody else on the trip, George included.

Kit nodded. "The cave network could be miles long."

The breeze excited them, perhaps more than it might have if they'd found anything noteworthy in their test pits. It was decided that George would borrow Mark's flashlight and venture into the dark zone to see if he could find the source of the wind, and Kit would accompany him. Mark and Val would stay behind, in case anything went wrong.

After the others had gone, Mark and Val worked in silence for some minutes, scraping their trowels methodically and removing loose dirt more thoroughly than they usually did. Val was more engrossed by this task than attentive to it, and as she reached the edge of the pit, she scraped her hand against a rock protruding from the baulk. She brought her hand to her mouth instinctively, sucking away dirt along with her blood.

"You should put some iodine on that," said Mark.

"Well." This would have been the end of it, but after a pause she continued. "That was weird, right? The cave, I mean."

Mark shook his head. "Atmospheric pressure."

"I know. But it was like it was breathing."

⚘

Three days earlier, Kit had called Min-Seo from Vasiliy's house and talked briefly about nothing. The baby was sleeping, and she didn't want to wake him. When they hung up, he'd considered calling his parents but decided against it. They'd grown depressing since retirement. His father, once widely renowned for his work in particle physics and implicitly feared within his department for the Machiavellian maneuvers that had positioned him as its head, now spent all his time building birdhouses. Not even new or interesting birdhouses, because his interest lay not in architecture but in the manipulation of materials. So he built essentially the same birdhouse over and over again, now in cedar, now in bamboo, testing wood flexibility and durability and the esoteric preferences of the birds.

Whenever his son came to visit, Kit's father would rant about his dealings with the incompetent clerk at King's Hardware, or with the Lorenzos across the street, who refused to put a bell on their cat, or with the rain, before sensing Kit's disinterest, making some sour remark, and sending him off abruptly with a birdhouse in his arms. Kit kept them stacked in a coat closet to regift when the occasion arose. He'd given one to Mark last Christmas, after drawing his name in a mandatory Secret Santa exchange. Mark had been confused but complimented the craftsmanship. In any case, if his mother picked up, it would be manageable, but there was no telling how long his father would want to talk if he was the one to answer, and it would be rude to run up long-distance calls on a stranger's phone.

The current coolness between Kit and George arose only after George had invited him on the expedition and, in a strange and indirect way, stemmed from Kit's father. They had never been close.

Kit rejected George's paternalism, and George chafed against Kit's way of addressing him as an equal, but they had the mutual respect of competence recognizing competence. Though neither liked the other very much on a personal level, each assumed that the other liked him. This was basically the same as genuine good feeling, at least where career-oriented people are involved.

But once he picked Kit for the trip, the power games began. George operated like a Mafia boss. When he saw he could not instill loyalty in Kit, he tried to subdue him through obligation. Kit understood the tactic, and George understood that he understood. This only compounded the tension. And then there had been that argument after the Christmas party. He'd made an enemy then, he felt certain. And now George was resorting to scare tactics.

Kit didn't consider himself a fearful person generally, but the instinct to shiver as they ventured farther into the dark zone proved inescapable. George's flashlight illuminated only a circle of damp earth in front of them, giving no hint as to how long the walkable corridor continued. Worse, he had no idea how far away the walls and ceiling of the cave were, whether they were creeping inward to suffocate him or drifting away to leave him unmoored in the center of a black hole.

Kit didn't even have his own flashlight on hand and was dependent on George's steady, indifferent hand. He figured out that the passage was narrowing only when a wet wall scraped his arm, forcing him in line behind George, who occasionally held his flashlight out at a distance in front of him, trying for a wider view of what lay ahead. The first two times he did this, the light dissipated slowly into dark, revealing nothing. On the third, it showed the results of an internal avalanche blocking up the passage.

George increased his pace, forcing Kit to stride to keep up. But once he realized the game—there seemed to be no end to George's games, even here in the pits of Hell—he forced himself to slow down. George and his light moved ahead, leaving Kit swallowed by darkness for a few dreadful moments, but he followed the light and reached the rocks soon after. George was already inspecting them. "Calcite buildup."

Kit could see that for himself. The passage had fallen in on itself thousands of years ago, and calcium drip had softened the rocks' edges, glued them together, and filled up some of the smaller gaps between them. Large cracks ran through the calcite buildup, though, as if it had been pulled apart. There was an opening at the top where the rocks were smaller, large enough to peer through. This was the focus of George's interest. Kit ran his hand along one of the cracks, and George looked sharply down at him.

"The rocks almost look like they've been moved," said Kit.

George shook his head. "There was a major earthquake in the area some years back. We're near a fault line."

Kit nodded slowly. An earthquake could certainly have made cracks in the calcite buildup, but the pattern here looked too deliberate, too evenly distributed, too focused on the rocks that would need to be moved in order to pass through. It seemed not unlikely that other explorers had come before them, a dispiriting prospect. Though, it occurred to him, who would bother to put the rocks back in place when they'd finished?

"Okladnikov surveyed the area when?"

"1963. Briefly. There's no record of any excavation here, and I don't see how they could have transported the equipment. This was an earthquake."

To George this settled the matter. He looked back to the opening at the top of the avalanche, shined his light through it. After a moment, he motioned for Kit to look. Not much of the next chamber was visible. The rocks had fallen in such a way that only a sliver of the left wall was visible, at an awkward angle. But on this sliver, a series of diagonal black streaks could be seen. They were thick, very distinct, and evenly spaced. They seemed, from what little they could see, as if they might be man-made. The two men looked at each other in surprise, then Kit watched as George's expression morphed into one of analysis. He looked Kit up and down. "You're about five foot nine?"

"Ten."

"How much do you weigh?"

Kit didn't respond, and after a moment, George shook his head. He looked ghoulish in the beam of artificial light. Kit thought of Val, the night before: *We could tell ghost stories!*

"I'd go myself," said George, "but the opening is too small."

Kit shook his head and turned to leave, but as George made no motion to follow, he was forced to turn around after a few steps. "I'd never go in there without clearing the rocks first. They could collapse, or you might get stuck. It's too much of a risk."

"In any case, you wouldn't fit. The hole narrows a bit."

Kit nodded and waited for George to take some measurements and note them down before they began to walk back.

They didn't speak for a while, and Kit focused his energy on trying not to look behind him. He felt watched. George, now by his side in the widened corridor, wasn't watching him, though. He was looking straight ahead and, inexplicably, smiling.

"It will be interesting to see what's behind there," said Kit, "once we get the Russians in to move the debris."

"The Russians," said George contemptuously, still smiling.

"If there are paintings, they'll pay to clear the way."

George turned to him then. His face was a mask, but his eyes burned through it. "If we wait for the Russians, they'll write us out of the story. It's our cave, and it's our find."

Kit didn't reply.

"Of course the rock bars won't be strong enough."

"No."

"If I'd brought some sort of winch, that could work."

"I can't imagine using one here. You could damage the structural integrity that way. You need professionals."

"Yes, we'll see."

"It's not safe."

"We'll figure something preliminary out. I'll ask around."

"What do you mean?"

"Maybe Val could fit through." All the excitement in George's voice had gone. He now spoke this casually, with a hint of irony, the way a person spoke at a dinner party rather than a dark cave.

Kit laughed. They walked for a minute in silence. Slowly, he realized George's tone of irony had been only to get Kit used to the idea. He was in fact entirely serious.

"With what equipment?" Kit asked sharply.

"We can just see if it's possible." The lightness in George's voice was maddening.

"She could *die.*"

George did not pause to consider this. "I chose my team for this expedition very carefully, with every contingency planned for. It's an incredibly important matter, for me, for you, for the field of archaeology, for—"

Kit exhaled audibly, cutting him off, but George ignored him and continued.

"Now, I value all three of you for your knowledge, but as you know, this job requires more than academic skill. You've got to be an outdoorsman, a radio technician, an accountant, a builder, a student of human nature; you've got to be *brave.* And any advantages you may have, be they mental or physical, you have to use them."

"This," said Kit, "is unprofessional."

⚘

George gave away nothing when they got back to the mouth of the cave, though Mark's and Val's questions were made out chiefly to him. Unwilling to enter into even a minor conspiracy with George, Kit told them that he'd made out the vague shadows of what might have been man-made markings on the wall behind the avalanche. Val needed to see them immediately. George said she couldn't, because the flashlight's batteries seemed to be low and the light had been flickering, a report that surprised Mark, who had changed the batteries before the trip with Duracell rather than a store brand. Val didn't mind going back to camp to grab another flashlight, and before George could come up with a new maneuver, Kit said, "Yes, let's go," and began to walk away.

"This is crazy," said Val, catching up to him. "Do you really think they're paintings?"

"I'm not sure."

"Well, what did you see? Geometric or representative? How big were they?"

"Just some lines. It was hard to see."

"But you thought they were man-made?"

"Maybe."

She looked up. "I'm not trying to bug you. It's just exciting."

"It is."

"You don't look excited. You look tense."

With a shrug, he attempted to unclench the muscles in his shoulders. "It's about George."

This had the effect of a light flicked off. "George?" She spoke coolly now, with forceful nonchalance.

"He told me something strange back there. The crevasse at the top of the debris? He was suggesting that we climb through it, but really he meant you."

Val exhaled in a strange, choppy way. It might have been a laugh. "But that's ridiculous. I could damage something, the paintings."

Kit expected an immediate defense, which he could then counter very gently, even agreeing if she said something true, like that George was intelligent or that he and Kit had some previous unresolved issues that might affect his interpretation. This would make him credible. But Val's response was surprisingly *professional*.

"You could be crushed."

"Well."

"No, really. You could. It's an unexplored collapsed passage. We have no idea how stable it is or how much it truly narrows, and you have no experience spelunking."

"I really think you must have misunderstood what he meant."

His frown deepened. She handed him a cigarette from a pack she must have stashed somewhere on her person and a grimy white Bic lighter. The cigarette was robin's-egg blue with a gold filter. He lit it and handed her back the lighter.

"Aren't these wonderful? Don't they make you feel like an exiled duke?" She took one out for herself, pink like soap.

"You wouldn't risk it, would you? If he asked?"

"He won't ask. He was making a joke."

"He said he brought you because you were small enough to slip through tight spaces."

"See, that's exactly what I mean. You don't get his humor. He was trying to joke around with you, to include you or thaw whatever psychological Cold War you two have going on—because it's honestly stressful to witness—and you took it in the worst possible way."

The walk was short, and they'd reached the camp, but neither went to retrieve a flashlight.

"I can tell when a person is joking."

"Can you? You never laugh."

"Because *you* never joke. You always actually mean it."

"Only sort of."

"But really, would you do it?"

She dropped her pink soap cigarette, only half smoked, and crushed it under the toe of her steel-toed boot. They weren't looking at each other, but he could feel her anger, see it in her body through the corner of his eye. Our ancestors had evolved this kind of subtle situational awareness to detect predators. In the modern man, it reemerged for petty fights.

"Jesus. You and Mark. It's like just because I'm not arguing over some stupid Jared Diamond that I didn't even read. I know neither of you even *read* that book, and I'm not pretending this is a hard science like I guess I'm supposed to."

"Oh, so now I'm a processualist?" He spat this out like a slur. Kit had not found comfort in objective truths since childhood.

"That's not even the point. You think I'm just an idiot? With no clue how to do my work and no respect for the field? My personal life—"

"Your personal life?" The thought came to him suddenly that she was sleeping with George. But she wouldn't. She really did care about the work. On the other hand, she might. She was careless, destructive. It was just like her to put him in that position. He took a last drag. "Really, Val, you don't help yourself."

"With what?"

This was not a question to answer, Kit knew. "Getting drunk at all the faculty parties, spilling wine."

"Because you're such a professional?"

"You're ridiculous because you don't take yourself seriously."

"And you're ridiculous because you do."

He laughed bitterly.

When they returned with flashlights, the group ventured back into the cave together. A silent exchange of excitement, suspicion, curiosity, and contempt passed between them as they walked, all except for Mark, who seemed preoccupied mostly with his physical discomfort as he navigated his large frame farther down the narrowing passage.

When he peered through the opening, Mark agreed that the lines looked like something, possibly, though he wasn't sure what, and it might be nothing. Val was too short to look through the gap, which even Kit had needed to stand on tiptoe to see. Nobody offered to help her, and she couldn't bring herself to ask, nor could she climb a foot up the rocks to get a look after her speech to Kit about her integrity and respect for the field and its rules and principles, so in the end, she didn't get a chance to form an opinion.

That night, dinner was a dull mix of plastic-wrapped camping food. The air was cooler than it had been, though the sun gave no indication that it felt inclined to set. Val and Kit sat quietly apart, and Mark's theories about the marks in the cave could fill only so much silence. George entertained them with a story about a coming-of-age ritual he'd witnessed in an isolated village on the Mongolian border where, when a boy reached a certain height, he was given a hallucinogenic brew called "dragon's milk," then placed in a cave too small to stand up in. A boulder would then be rolled in front of the cave, closing it off and leaving the boy with no light and limited air. He had to somehow dislodge the boulder on his own, emerging a man and leaving the old child self dead in the cave. Supposedly they'd let the boy suffocate if he wasn't strong enough, but no cases of death had occurred within living memory. Sometimes fathers and pitying uncles helped loosen the rock a bit from the outside.

Still, worse than a faulty battery. Mark said that really, if you can't even trust Duracell anymore, what can you trust? Outsourcing was the issue. Everything made in China. And then he looked guiltily at Kit, who hadn't been at all annoyed until he received this look, and shut up.

Citing mosquitoes, they disbanded quickly to read in their own tents.

Later in the persistent brightness of the evening, Val made peace, as she always did when they argued, by offering a cigarette. She had just one Sobranie left, and they shared it with stilted goodwill, talking around the point in a way he'd perfected with Min-Seo.

"I think," Val said, after ten minutes of nonsense, "we're all just tired. It's this crazy light. Makes everything just seem off."

They looked up at the pale purple sky, and the sky looked down on them serenely, without pity, making no attempt to defend itself.

The next week was spent in tension and drudgery. The feverish pace at which they'd begun had slowed. They dug methodically, photographing and storing possible artifacts, frequently measuring the depth of their pits. George spent some time digging with them and some alone at camp, working through maps and notes. Nothing of much interest was found, only a few animal bones possibly marked by blades, possibly by claws. Besides Mark, who was characteristically both suspicious and oblivious, they were all slightly more wary of one another.

Still, they saw themselves as professionals and worked efficiently.

The collapsed passage remained a point of contention, though an unspoken one. Kit watched to make sure that George didn't lead Val back or that Val didn't sneak off alone. He knew it was gnawing at her, the idea that everyone else had seen it but her, the one who was writing a dissertation on cave art. George watched Kit too. He didn't like to leave him alone with Val or even with Mark, though the latter figure should not have concerned him.

Mark, who could have been an ally if Kit had told him what was happening, got into a habit of humming "Greensleeves" as he worked. Whenever anybody asked him to stop, he'd say he hadn't realized he was doing it. What was worse, he seemed to know only a small part of the tune and hummed this fifteen seconds of medieval lute music on repeat for a week. Even when he dropped it, it would play in Kit's head. It crept into his dreams at night. Min-Seo, pregnant again, playing "Greensleeves" on a handheld radio against her stomach.

He dreamed about Val too. Weird sex dreams of Val with George. Val with his father. George with Min-Seo. George *as* his father, sitting behind his father's oak desk, offering him a drink and laughing maniacally when he took a sip. Mark walking in as he choked on the poison, whistling "Greensleeves."

Mark had grown irritating in a number of other ways, each innocuous on its own but building on one another to create an almost unbearable effect. He would read at lunch from a gigantic book about Joseph Stalin and underline sentences with a faulty ballpoint that scratched audibly along the pages. He had somehow lost his watch before they'd arrived. (According to Val, he had gambled it away in a card game.) Consequently, he would ask Kit for the time every hour, almost eerily on the hour. He bathed, it seemed, only every third day and developed an odor. Kit considered broaching the smell, but how could you tell a grown man to take a bath? Mark had taken to pacing at night too. A light sleeper, Kit saw him in silhouette against his tent at three in the morning, skulking.

On the morning of the seventh day of excavating they took no days off, having nothing else to do—Kit went down to the river to clean up. While his colleagues grew scruffy, Kit shaved every day. He didn't like the feeling of stubble and thought beards were only useful to lend a jawline or the illusion of seriousness to men who lacked these qualities, which he did not. He liked a clean profile, and he grew to like the river too.

He knew as well as any archaeologist that civilization sprung from fresh water, but before, rivers had only ever felt ornamental in his life. He'd walked along the Humber at sunset on his first date with Min-Seo, and it cast a dreamy tint over the memory of it: holding her hand in his, feeling her blood beat through her skin, the Humber guiding along them like fate. Or like love itself, or life, or death; the river could stand in for anything important. A grave, gentle, ancient creature. A slow but inexorable procession through the city.

This river was smaller, faster, fresher. It quickly became the center of his practical life on the expedition. George had said that when the undergrads came, they'd filter it for drinking water to offset the expense of hydrating dozens of bourgeois teens performing manual labor, but even now it was indispensable. They all bathed in the river, at a bend where it grew wide and shallow, and washed their clothes in it, hanging them up to dry on twine strung through the trees. He performed this ritual more often than the others. Having grown to find comfort in the smell of minerals and soap in his freshly cleaned and sun-dried clothes, he got into the habit of changing his shirts at lunchtime. Really, everybody should have been doing so—they were all sweating heavily in the wet heat—but George, with mixed admiration, called him fastidious. Val said he was a dandy. She was trying to joke with him like she used to, but the gesture felt forced, and he smiled only out of pity. Too much had been said, and they couldn't be natural around each other anymore.

It was partly to avoid her that he began to wake up early to shave at the river, though routine and solitude also played into it. He'd sit and run his hands through the moss, watch the play of light on the rippling water, close his eyes and listen to its movements. But he wasn't used to the wilderness and didn't understand it. He heard sounds sometimes and didn't know enough to attribute them to one cause or another. That morning, he noticed something: dirt spread out in a zigzag line between trees. He crouched to examine it: an almost deliberate pattern, as if somebody had mussed it to cover up their footprints.

When he returned, Kit found Mark alone at breakfast, underlining passages in *STALIN*. He pointedly did not ask about George and Val when he returned, but Mark miserably volunteered the information that they'd gone up to the cave early to photograph the pits. This was wholly unnecessary, as the pits were photographed throughout the day. Kit knew it was a lie and considered pursuing them, if only to protect the integrity of the site. But then he felt too unnerved to go up alone and too embarrassed at this feeling to admit it to himself.

He brought the zigzag line up to Mark, who said that it was probably nothing, a deer or other large animal. But the confidence in his tone was too brittle to reassure. And what was it Vasiliy's wife had said? *Occupied.* For a moment, he thought Mark might offer to have a look, but instead he went back to *STALIN*, clicking a pen to the rhythm of "Greensleeves," accurately enough that Kit would have been impressed had he not wanted to strangle him.

"Could you not, with the pen?" he asked, as neutrally as he could manage.

"Oh, sorry." He went back to his book and, after a minute, to clicking the pen. Kit cleared his throat, and Mark set the pen down in his lap.

Kit ate his granola without pleasure, looking at the dirt. Mark, after a few minutes, shut the book.

"I can't read it without the pen," he said.

"Oh."

"It's funny. In a way, there's a lot to admire about Stalin. He came from nothing. His parents were serfs."

"Well," said Kit. He was mimicking Val, and they both realized it after he'd said it.

Mark picked up his pen. "I've been debating whether or not to bring something up. It's . . ."

"What?"

"Them. George and Val."

"What about them?"

"I know she's got that free spirit thing," said Mark, clicking, "that, I don't know, emotional thing, but I didn't think she'd go this far. I mean, is she just that impulsive, or what does she want? Does she think this will help her career? Do you remember what happened with Jennifer? Remember Jennifer Blumbach, with Dr. Brady? She was a *joke*. She had to get a job in an *office*. She works with *foreclosed homes.* And Val knows Jennifer. She knows all of that. So what's the angle? It's so . . . it's *disgusting*." With that, he fell silent.

"Did she actually talk to you about it?" Kit asked after a moment.

"She didn't *tell* me, obviously. But I see her at night. She walks past my tent to get to his. I see her shadow pass by. She must know I can see her."

"Is that," Kit ventured, "why you've been pacing?"

"Have I been pacing? I've been distracted."

"At night."

They fell into silence, both gazing in the direction of the cave.

"It's shameful," Mark said after a moment, his voice strained. "I really didn't expect it of her."

"And him?" asked Kit.

"He's European, so . . ."

"Sort of." Kit shrugged. You could never tell what would embarrass somebody. And Mark was particularly susceptible to useless, paranoid shame over his own behaviors, though the application of this shame was inconsistent. If he could, Kit would have tried to redirect it toward "Greensleeves."

"But really, what are you talking about? With the pacing at night?" Mark asked, sounding genuinely perplexed.

"I've seen you," said Kit. He looked at Mark as he spoke, and Mark looked at him. Neither enjoyed this eye contact, but they were men, they had their dignity. "Your silhouette at night."

"I don't pace at night."

"Oh."

Each picked up his backpack, and Kit said, "Maybe it was somebody else." The absurdity of this hung dead in the air for a moment, and then they began their silent walk to the cave.

They worked more efficiently that morning than usual, each trying to prove to the rest that he was a professional, an impartial tool for the furthering of humanity's collective knowledge. They weren't silent either. That would be an admission. Instead, they reviewed protocol more than was necessary, asking questions they knew the answers to ("The brushes are in the blue bag?") and remarking on the lack of differentiation in the sediment layers. Nobody attempted a joke or the introduction of any topic of conversation not directly related to the cave.

By lunch, Kit noticed his jaw was sore from unconscious clenching. He asked Val for a cigarette, but she'd run out. "Well," she said, "except for the Belomors."

"You kept the Belomors?"

She nodded gravely, and they walked back to camp to retrieve them.

"You were up early." He couldn't help but say this, once they were out of earshot.

9

Val didn't trust Lily's advice per se. She had nobody in her life whom she trusted for advice. Still, she wanted to talk to her sister. Lily wouldn't tell her she'd made a mess of things. Lily had a sense of adventure. She said a lie counted only when the person you were lying to actually deserved the truth, which was almost never. She thought Val was the responsible one.

And compared with Lily, Val really was responsible. Growing up, she'd done the laundry and dishes while Lily lay on the couch nursing hangovers, watching sitcoms with interchangeable delinquent boyfriends, tripping LSD patterns on the ceiling and trying unsuccessfully to describe them. Their father always found some pretext to stay longer at work or to dwell on it when he finally did come home. (Val would complain about this as a child, but people said she should be grateful he had chosen to raise them himself. Whatever it was that unexpectedly single men did to dispose of their children—send them off to starve to death in a forest, or to scrub floors for some sadistic great-aunt, or to foster care, military school, or trafficking rings—was implied rather than stated. The concept of gratitude turned reasonable through repetition, and she stopped complaining, became the responsible one.)

She hadn't resented it much either. For one thing, service earned love. The Howes were an intermittently demonstrative group of people, and both father and sister would occasionally be moved almost to tears by a well-timed cup of tea. There was comfort too in knowing the right thing to do. Vinegar and detergent could get red wine out of the carpet, but you had to dab, never scrub. Wash sheets in hot water, clothing in cold. Play upbeat music to get the dishes done faster. With nobody to teach her, she worked hard to learn these secrets, and they took on a vague but deeply felt philosophical significance. Stain removal and the meaning of life.

But Val was never a homebody, exactly. Being the younger sister, she was often roped into Lily's schemes and adventures. She took her to strange places, gave her strange drinks and pills and cigarettes, introduced her to strangers. And this was important. Val wouldn't have cared about stain removal if she couldn't make the stains. But cleanliness, some semblance of order, the assurance that she could get things done when necessary, underpinned her strange life with Lily.

Then she went off to college, Lily split for LA, and these two sides of her—the side that spilled and the side that cleaned—became less complementary, less easily compartmentalized. There didn't seem to be a right thing to do anymore. Any gesture toward happiness or harmony ended up a tangle of contradictions.

That was what drew her to George. He never contradicted himself. He made so much sense that she couldn't help but make sense herself, when she was with him. She'd wanted more of that and ended up making an even bigger mess than the one she'd left behind. Lily, she knew, would make all of this seem picaresque, if she could only talk to her.

The satellite phone could reach any phone in the world, but it was meant for emergencies only and stored in its own tent at the center of their little camp. She'd have to wait another two days until they went back to Yakutsk for the weekend.

After that first night with George, she slunk away before Mark and Kit woke up, but George had already gone. He'd left her clothes folded at the bottom of the mat. She figured she'd driven him away. Sleeping next to another person was horrible under any circumstances. The space they took up, the way they anchored the blankets, their shifting legs, the consciousness that you were not, as a person practicing for death should be, alone. And the summer heat made it worse. She wouldn't ask where he'd gone or stay until morning again.

That day, he treated her as he always did. She'd half expected him to ignore her completely, but this happy impartiality was somehow worse. He joked with her as lightly as he always had and consulted her as much as he always did, and never met her eye in a secret way, and asked Kit to go with him to look for the source of the wind in the cave. She didn't seek him out the next night or the night after that, even after he'd rested his hand on her shoulder while looking over her test pit that afternoon. She got as far as lacing her boots up that night before a sudden sensation of self-awareness compelled her to unlace them again. But last night, when the sun had sunk as low as it ever did in the subarctic summer sky and the camp was silent, George came to her.

She had imagined herself saying, *You should go.* But he said her name so well. "Valerie, I need your help."

He talked the whole time, as he led her up to the cave. She liked to listen to him, but still felt uneasy. Prescience curled through the air. Omen quelled the wind. She wished, for a moment, that Mark was there to give another lesson on atmospheric pressures. George did not explain what he needed her for, exactly, but instead told a story.

"You know, after I left the Soviet land survey, I spent some time with the Buryats and some time with the Yakuts."

"What?" The limestone cliff face loomed black above them. The trees behind them, however, reflected some secondhand light from the moon, and their soft glow creeped into her peripheral vision. She felt watched.

"After I—"

"Oh, right. Yes."

"When I joined the Yakuts, they told me of a valley of ghosts where no living man is allowed to go. Of course I had to see it. Ghost stories are often attributed to rich archaeological sites."

"Konstantin Krovaviy," said Val.

"For example."

George had told her before about the discovery of the Venus of Konstantin Krovaviy cave, a thirty-thousand-year-old carved sculpture found by a student of Okladnikov in a supposedly haunted cave by a small village near Lipetsk. A local man had warned him that the cave had once been inhabited by an aesthetic monk named Konstantin, whom the devil had seduced into sacrificing a child in exchange for arcane knowledge. The cave led to Hell if you crawled in far enough, and Konstantin's ghost lurked near the mouth, trying to lure in passersby.

"Is our cave supposed to lead to Hell?"

"They only said in a general way that it was haunted. 'Haunted' isn't even the correct translation. But in any case, I managed to contract two young men to lead me into the valley in exchange for gold. I always carry gold. Everybody takes it. That's a lesson from my father, from the diplomatic service. The men brought me to the edge of the valley but refused to go down into it, even for double the pay. There were two of them and only one of me, and we were very far from any other people, so I couldn't refuse payment even though they'd reneged. I paid them half and told them to wait three days for me. If I gave myself too much time, I thought I'd likely get lost or the men would grow impatient and leave. Even three days were dangerous. I knew very little about navigation at that time, but I'd come all that way, and the young are reckless. I'd been driven half wild by disappointment. And being entirely alone, with no other living person around for miles, it had a certain effect on the psyche.

"On the first day, I found nothing. The valley being as narrow as it is, I decided to stay in between the mountains, where the men were waiting, and the river. I cut an X into a tree every now and again to mark my path, but this was done haphazardly. I've always had a good memory and a good sense of direction. I relied on these skills with complete abandon. The whole expedition, really, was done in the stupidest possible way."

"I can't imagine it."

"You should have seen me. Really, I do wish I'd known you then."

She had been in the first grade when he abandoned the Soviet land survey, but didn't point this out.

"About halfway through the second day, I realized how pointless the whole endeavor was, conducted in that way. I still had some tarasun, a sort of fermented goat's milk, highly hallucinogenic when brewed through a certain process, from my time with the Buryats. It had gone a bit off, or more off than it was supposed to be, but I decided to drink it anyway."

"Oh."

"You think I'm mad. Maybe I was. I can't describe the mindset I was in at the time. But understand this: my whole life, I'd been building upward toward a goal, and then, suddenly, I was struck down, reduced to chaos, rubble. That summer I kept talking about the Tower of Babel, but the Yakuts didn't understand. They'd never read the Bible; Christianity never took root here, although the czar sent missionaries along as he built the railroad. A tale of intentional suffering in a temperate climate simply held no interest for them. But I had no other metaphor by which to explain myself. It was the only time in my life when I felt that nothing held the world together."

"I always feel like that."

"History. History holds the world together."

They had reached the cave and now stood at its mouth. Cool air pushed out to touch them, and with their eyes now adjusted to the low light, the darkness in front of them made the rock of the cliffside look light by comparison. George paused only for a second, then walked onward. Val followed, focusing on the small patch of flashlit dirt in front of her feet as she moved.

"So what happened?"

"I had a vision. By the river, I saw a man. I walked toward him, and he toward me. He looked strange, not like any man I'd seen before. I touched his face, and he touched mine, and we stared at each other. His face changed, and then we were fighting. I can't explain it any clearer than that. This all happened too quickly for me to recall it with any precision.

"He was very strong and would have beaten me to death if I'd tried just to match him blow for blow. We were about half a mile upstream from where the camp is now, where the river is wide and shallow enough to bathe. I backed away from him, toward the edge of the water, then lunged and dragged him in with me. I intended to drown him, but it takes a long time to drown a man, and he was strong. I held him down for a while and then he held me down, I think. The water was above me, but below me there were no rocks, only light. I tried to swim toward it, but ended up above water again, gasping for air. We'd tumbled downstream, where the current was quicker, but not strong enough to sweep you away if you could swim. The man could not swim, it seemed. He clung to a rock. I swam to the opposite bank of the river and climbed up. I called out to the man that I would save him, in English at first, then Russian, then broken Yakut, then French and Italian, although I can't think why. He understood nothing.

"It's a tricky thing to save a drowning man. He'll panic and pull you under with him, especially if you have no way of communicating with him. I had a length of rope in my bag, back on the bank about fifty meters away. I had to run for it, as it was impossible to tell how long he'd be able to hold his grasp on the rock. The ground seemed to sink beneath my feet and rise upward in waves in front of me, and the branches of the pines reached out like the arms of needy children, trying to grab me. The dried pine needles cracked so loudly as I walked, and the river pounded against the rocks like beating blood."

Val didn't know what to say, so she stayed silent as he led her farther through the dark.

"That is, I was still experiencing strong hallucinations. I went to knot the rope around the trunk of a tree on the bank near where the man was drowning, but the rope kept wriggling out of my hands like a snake, and any knot untied itself before I could tighten it. Eventually I managed to attach it, though how securely, I couldn't say. I placed a rock onto the loose end of the rope to weigh it down and threw it out to the man. He caught it and, in doing so, lost his grip on the rock. This sent him into a flailing, screaming panic, and I had to wade out into the water myself to show him how to pull himself up to land with the rope. I did get him out eventually. Thank God the knot held. I didn't think then that it would. We lay together, exhausted on the bank, for some time. Adrenaline can drain very quickly once it's no longer needed and leave you with absolutely nothing. We fell asleep, and when I woke up, there were more of these strange men."

"Strange?"

"They had unusual features. Very large eyes, like the eyes of children. They had . . . they led me to this cave. It was still light out, but the sun was finally near to setting. They lit torches at the mouth of the cave and walked in. I followed, still seeing patterns in the dark, and their fire seemed to bloom and wilt over and over again, like a flower growing and dying and growing up again ten times in a minute. When we reached the avalanche . . ." He turned to her. They had, as if he'd planned it, just reached the avalanche themselves.

He loved telling her stories of his adventures, and she loved to listen, but he always positioned himself as the straight man, curious, easy to convince but difficult to shake; a person for whom things seemed to happen, around whose solidity chaos orbited but could never puncture. Having expected a story like that, she didn't know what to make of this one.

His light shone on the fallen rocks, and his voice moved through the cavern on its own, his face cloaked entirely in darkness. She wanted to point her flashlight at him, to tap on his shoulder so he'd turn around. Then she could get a read on his expression. She was close enough. She could reach out and touch him.

"One of the men handed me his torch, and the other two set theirs down, allowing the flames to die. The smoke made me cough, but the others didn't seem to mind it. They were, as I said, very strong. The man I had fought and the other men too. And together, they lifted the rocks, cleared them all away." He moved his light up and down the central crack in the calcium holding the avalanche together. Smaller cracks, like tributaries, fed into it, where, if he was telling the truth, the rocks had been lifted.

"I thought at first that Mark might be of some use in moving the rocks, but I see now that even if I'd brought five Marks, they'd be too heavy. It was stupid, really, but I had only memory to rely on, and they'd made it look so easy."

"What did you see? Behind the rocks. What did they show you?"

He waved his flashlight upward, toward the hole at the top of the collapse. "I've measured this, and I think you could fit."

Her first instinct was to laugh, but she quelled this, then raised her eyes to the hole above her head.

"How wide are your hips?" he asked.

"I don't know."

"You don't know your measurements? You've never had a dress made?"

"No."

He looked her up and down, calculating. "I think you should fit."

"Shouldn't we wait?"

"If we wait for the Russians, it's theirs. Val," he said, and was then on his knees, his hands on her shoulders, his handsome features glowing in the light and his eyes looking up at her, searching, burning. "Things aren't always done the way they're taught in school. People, real people, the people whose names are remembered—they know when to disregard protocol. This is a chance to *do something*."

She didn't have the composure to keep her face a mask. She knew that she couldn't leave now. That he knew her better than she'd thought he did. That she'd walked into the darkness with him, and it was against her nature to walk back alone. She nodded.

It's very rare for a life-altering decision to be made consciously. Usually it's only in retrospect that the scope of a choice's consequences becomes clear. Still, a sudden but conscious alteration in circumstance or position happens once or twice in every life. Val saw that this was one of those occasions and felt its significance. She wanted to take a moment to sit in this significance, but practical considerations intruded. She was wearing pajama shorts and an old T-shirt that pictured a bloated and wild-eyed cartoon penguin flapping its wings and screaming, through a zagzag speech bubble, LOTSA THINGS TO DO AT THE RIVERVIEW ZOO!

George claimed he'd told her to change before they left, but she had no memory of this. He gave her a headlamp he had stashed away that, though necessary, made her feel ridiculous as she fastened it around her forehead. "Indiana Jones," she said.

He took off his button-down and gave it to her, so she could shield her arms at least. She wanted his jacket instead, as it was thicker, but he said it would bulk her up, and the passage was already a tight fit. After a short negotiation, she pulled her socks up to cover most of her calves, and he helped lift her toward the opening.

The rocks held their place as she stepped from one to another, and the climb was not a difficult one, only a few feet high and slanted slightly, with the rocks wedged firmly against one another. The difficulty came with the hole. It was longer than she'd expected, about three feet of rock to work through before reaching the antechamber. When she looked through, she saw what had first excited the others so much. Three thick black streaks, smeared diagonally across the left face. They curved slightly at the bottom, but whatever they curved into was tantalizingly obscured by the claustrophobic maze of fallen rocks between them.

She managed to squeeze in past her waist before the trouble began. The passage curved slightly at that point, and there was not enough space to shift her body in order to fit it. She tried, felt the rocks cut into her thin clothes, and stilled. She adjusted to a new intensity of spatial awareness. The rocks were all around her, sharp, wet, heavy, and pointing inward toward her body.

"It's not going to work," she called out. The words echoed around her.

There was no reply for a moment. She tried to wiggle backward, repeating the statement.

"Just try," said George.

She paused, then did so. Having moved back a few inches, she could bend slightly in anticipation of the curve and managed to get a little farther this time. The pointed edge of an outcropping of rock dug into her forearm, and she ignored it until it sliced the skin. She gasped in pain, felt the warm wet of her blood mingle with the cold wet of the passage, tried to move backward. This pressed the blade of rock only farther into her arm. It was positioned against the side of her arm, thankfully, not close to a vein, but it sliced deep. She couldn't turn her head to see the mess.

"Just try," George said again, when she hadn't moved for a minute.

"It hurts."

"Can you see it?"

"No. There's a rock covering everything." This was true. From her current angle, she could see only the wet black rock of the bend in the passage.

She tried to move backward again, and a pebble fell from above. Her arm stung, and she could feel the trickle of blood seeping out from it.

"Is there an issue?" asked George. She pictured a rock tumbling down, caving her head in like a fruit, and couldn't respond. She tried to wiggle another inch backward and found that she could not.

"I'm stuck."

"Just try."

"I can't. I'm stuck. I need you to pull me out, to just—" Her voice rose with panic, but stopped when she felt his hands on her ankles. She realized she hadn't been sure he would help her.

He pulled her out quickly, not giving her any time to adjust, like a doctor giving a shot. The rocks scraped against her temple, cheek, ribs, hip. The cut in her arm ripped open even more. She fell backward, gasping, insensible, and found herself sitting in the dirt. George knelt down beside her.

They were silent.

Eventually Val stood, and George said, "We can try again tomorrow, after chiseling off that sharp outcropping."

She turned around, pointing her headlight in his face. "You're crazy!"

After saying this, she began to cry and turned to leave him before he could leave her.

But he caught hold of her shoulder, gently, and kissed her. Not on the lips, but on her scraped temple, standing behind her. It was a tender gesture. She said, "That was so stupid."

"It was a bad plan."

"Yes."

"I'll get a winch when we go back to Yakutsk. You don't have to worry about it."

"Okay."

"But you should have told me when you got hurt."

"I tried to. I don't know."

A growing gang of mosquitoes circled Val and attempted to latch on to her skin as they walked back to camp. They seemed not to notice the cut on her arm, which was still bleeding, but George gave her his jacket to protect it anyway. This sent most of them down to bite at her legs, while a few of the larger, more vicious insects stayed and attempted to pierce through the light fleece. "They really do love you." George watched as she continued to swat at them.

"What was in there?" she asked.

He took a second to respond. "I wasn't clear minded at the time. It's hard to say."

"But what?"

"I can't explain it now." He gave her one of his hand-rolled cigarettes, with tobacco from the Caribbean, paper from France. She smoked it so quickly she felt sick. When they arrived back at camp, Val turned to the left at the satellite radio to go back to her tent, but George told her to wait.

"I'll wash this," she said, gesturing to the jacket. Her cut had begun to congeal, and the dried blood glued the jacket to her arm.

"I can put some iodine on the cut."

She allowed herself to be led back to his tent. The iodine stung and left an orange stain. He covered it in cotton gauze and undressed her. She felt like a ghost in her own body.

She woke up early and alone, left a note for George, and walked up to the caves before Kit and Mark gathered for breakfast. George joined her first. He said he'd run into Mark by the firepit, and he'd be up soon. He didn't have to tell her not to talk, acknowledging the night before only by an approving look at her long-sleeved shirt.

10

"Aren't you hot in that?" Kit asked, as he and Val attempted the Belomors at lunch. She hadn't responded to his earlier jab about rising early. This one was less direct. He really didn't know why she was wearing a long-sleeved shirt in the midday heat, but he felt it had something to do with George.

"I feel fine."

"It's ninety degrees out."

"Probably have malaria. I can never remember those pills."

"Me neither. I don't really see the point. But really, that looks uncomfortable."

"Well, not everyone does their laundry daily. I'm running low."

"Hm," said Kit.

"You have something else on your mind."

This was true. She could read him pretty well. But he wasn't talking to her like that anymore. She was on George's side now. Not to be trusted. He thought to mention the strange patterns he'd seen on the forest floor, to ask what animal might have made them. But something stopped him from speaking about it, and he couldn't think of anything else to say.

"These are terrible," she said, inhaling.

"Yeah," he replied, blowing smoke.

The test pits had yielded some evidence of habitation already, but excepting the possible paintings behind the avalanche, the results of the dig had been sparse and unremarkable. The few stone tools they'd discovered had been common throughout the paleolithic, and, devoid of organic material, they couldn't be dated through radiocarbon. Many sites were like this, occupied but lacking in any clear pattern, with holes in their stories larger than the stories themselves. But most sites were accessible by road or rail and did not require a specially hired Soviet crop duster to reach them. Their efforts had not yet been rewarded.

Nobody said this aloud. It wasn't in the culture of the profession to whine. Complaints looked unprofessional, ungrateful. Kit thought to mention that the pit he was digging in the twilight zone seemed pointless, as it was clear that the light zone held the vast majority of artifacts here, and in fact he'd found nothing but squirrel bones that may have been brought back by any cave-dwelling predator over the last fifty thousand years. But then he thought of his first dig as an undergraduate, where he'd seen a girl fake heatstroke in order to get out of working in the sun. On a dig, whiners were worse than murderers. And besides, communication had broken down among them.

The previous evening, he wrote in a letter to his wife that he was surrounded by lunatics in the Arctic Circle. He felt uneasy about the idea that he might in any way need to depend upon these people.

The older he got, the more he understood the value of normality. All his life, he had been drawn to people who said unusual things, made strange choices. He had been cursed from birth with a perceptive nature and knew what most people would say before they opened their mouths, more or less. Surprising encounters, for years, were all that kept him from fatalism.

But people who said unusual things, who made strange choices, were also far more likely to violate the broadly accepted standards of decency that kept society from total collapse. Normal wasn't normal arbitrarily. Normal was the only guide offered in a universe of accelerating entropy. People who tried to be different were not brave. They were arrogant, desperate, and confused. They made him miss his wife.

Because Min-Seo was different. She acted with intention. He'd been drawn to her based on an opposing instinct within him, one which craved clarity. He wrote this too, in another letter. He had a bundle of them, all addressed to his wife, to drop off at the post office when they returned to Yakutsk for supplies in a few days. But as the time neared, he became less sure that he wanted to send any of them. She had not been thrilled about this strategic career choice and might not want the details of its failure.

He'd buy her a diamond. A big one, perfectly cut and perfectly clear. All Russian diamonds were mined in Yakutia, and Vasiliy had told him you could buy them up cheap in Yakutsk from some of the less scrupulous Alrosa men, if you knew where to ask. He'd bring it up again when he saw him next. For now, he'd keep to himself.

After a lunch of trail mix and three-quarters of a Belomor, he returned to his pit before the others. The pits were all supposed to be dug a meter down. He'd dug down over half of this depth already and wanted to be done with the fruitless area he'd been assigned by the end of the day. Val and Mark joined him soon afterward. Work was preferable to attempting conversation. They'd begun the excavation process with two people per pit, to oversee each other's work and move faster through the division of labor. Now, each dug their own pit, having gradually drifted apart to maintain their sanity. He found another squirrel vertebrae, begrudgingly photographed it in situ, and then, an inch down, saw what at first looked to be a bone from a bat's wing.

But it came to a sharp point at one end, and when he looked more closely, a small hole had been drilled into the other end. It *was* drilled, too uniform and sharp at the edges to be organic. A shiver ran through him, but he brushed around it until the edges were distinct and photographed it before calling out, "George, come look at this."

George came to look, and Mark and Val came with him. They must have heard something in his voice. He'd tried to keep his pitch from rising and, in doing so, spoke in the low, deliberate tone of a prayer.

Crouching around the pit, they all stared at it, reverently, for almost a minute. Carved from bone and perfectly sharpened, with an evenly drilled hole, only about a millimeter wide. It seemed so unlikely. Mark broke the silence.

"A needle," he said, rather stupidly. Because of course it was a sewing needle. In design, it looked exactly the same as a modern sewing needle, except that it was made from bone instead of metal.

"It's so *deep*. What layer?" asked Val.

Mark shook his head. "The layers aren't precise here. Badgers."

"Badgers?"

"You know, they overturn the earth, they mess up the strata in caves."

"I don't see any badgers, or claw marks, or anything. I don't even think there are any badgers this far north."

"Not a single badger for the entirety of the Holocene?"

"The *Holocene*? Did you see how *deep*?"

"And not a single badger?"

"We'll send it for carbon dating, of course," said George, ending the argument. And then, to Kit, "But if the layers *are* intact . . ."

"About fifty thousand years."

They stayed and watched as Kit gently pried it from the ground with brushes and dental tools. Afterward, though they knew it was wrong, they passed it around so everybody could hold it. The implications of a fifty-thousand-year-old sewing needle would be seminal, if indeed that was what they'd found. Kit cautioned that stratigraphy (dating objects based on how deeply buried they were) was unreliable and that these layers were too sparse in artifacts to even achieve the level of accuracy a relative dating method like stratigraphy could provide. Mark brought up the badgers again.

But the needle didn't need to be fifty thousand years old for the find to be significant. *Homo sapiens* reached the northern edges of Siberia only thirty thousand years ago, at the earliest. Neanderthals had been there for hundreds of thousands of years by then. If the needle was even close to as old as it seemed, one of two possibilities must be true. The first would be that *Homo sapiens* migrated much earlier than previously thought. Otherwise, it meant that the thick-skulled, heavy-browed Neanderthal was capable of drilling a millimeter-wide eye into a bone needle and had thread to sew with and, if not fabric, then furs to shape into sewn garments. And it meant that Neanderthals had learned these skills before we did.

They made no pretense of working for the rest of the day, instead talking about the needle and its implications, George and Val making sweeping conclusions while Mark and Kit felt some obligation to counsel patience. They didn't really believe it, though. They all seemed to know that they'd found something big. And in finding it together and knowing it together, illogically, and without proper evidence, they were all suddenly very close friends.

Over dinner, they all laughed uproariously over George's story about trying to find a room for the night in Skopje. He'd been directed first to a whorehouse and then sent next door, to the run-down apartment of a pair of Mormon missionaries, who offered to let him stay the night. They gave him tea, he told them he was an archaeologist, and they explained how it had been proven that dinosaurs were a hoax. He thanked them very warmly, then went back to the whores.

Kit told George that he'd been thinking a lot about George's new book, about the Neanderthal brain size and self-domestication. That there might be something to it. Mark even smiled when Val attributed a rustling in the forest to a badger.

Before bed, Kit went to the garden shed where they'd been keeping the artifacts and held his needle again. It wasn't *his* needle, of course. It belonged to the Russian government and would be attributed as a discovery of "Professor George Auberon, PhD, Department of Archaeology, University of Toronto, and team." But that team consisted of only three people, of which he was the furthest along in his doctoral career. He'd present a paper on it, talk about implications, temporal and geographical connections. He'd start off, as people sometimes did, with an anecdote about the discovery.

When an archaeologist uncovered a historically significant artifact himself, he would usually start off his presentation with an anecdote. It helped ingratiate him with his audience and was the only opportunity he had to show that he'd found his treasure with his own hands, not through the unpaid labor of students. This was a distinction that was not supposed to matter but did. Unfortunately, most of these anecdotes went something along the lines of *I was digging in the ground, found nothing interesting for a while, and then chanced upon this unusual object*. This being essentially the process of all excavations, it was difficult to dramatize. Most would go the humor route, making some tepid jokes about blisters, heatstroke, and clueless undergrad volunteers before slipping in that they themselves had found the significant object. Kit had once seen a visiting professor, enamored of his own bass voice, attempt an inspirational approach, complete with dramatic pauses and a pantomimed reenactment of the moment of discovery.

Kit had always felt an aversion to occupational humor and had enough self-awareness not to try to inspire anybody either. But he did have other options. This dig in particular was so unusual that an account of its circumstances might be of some interest. But then, he realized, wasn't it all a bit *too* unusual? The tiny team, the lack of visibility, sleeping every other weekend in the arctic McMansion of a diamond oligarch? And where had the funding gone? He had been trying to ignore it, to push it down, this idea that George's methods would taint his own credibility. He'd have to lie, to leave things out. But these were problems to solve back in Canada. The find itself was miraculous.

When he left the shed, he saw Val smoking alone by the satellite radio. She held a delicate hand-rolled cigarette instead of the expected Belomor.

"You've been holding out on me," he said.

"When have I ever held out on you?"

She handed him the cigarette, and he took a drag. He was, in fact, hiding a Cuban cigar from her—a gift from Vasiliy—and smoking it by the river before she woke up. It tasted staler every morning but still beat the Belomors. Val, however, was always recklessly generous with her physical possessions. This had to be George's cigarette.

"Really, I'm hurt. I'd give you the shirt off my back, Kit." She put a hand to her heart.

"I prefer my own."

She laughed, called him bourgeois, and then asked, suddenly serious, "Aren't you excited?"

He turned to look at her. "Is that a trick question?"

"No. What would the trick be?"

"I don't know. I mean, yes, I'm excited." And then, willing to sound slightly stupid to repent for his suspicion, "Really, really excited."

Val took the cigarette back. "Me too."

He couldn't sleep for hours, thinking about the needle. Just as he drifted off, he saw Mark's large, slumping silhouette pass his tent. A strange person.

11

All day, abrupt, disconnected pebbles of memory fell around her. A hailstorm of useless information. Half-remembered facts from social issue documentaries, bad dates with high school crushes, snippets of song lyrics: *Stake me at the river, drop me in the water.*

But no. How did that song go? Lily would always sing the wrong words and make Val forget the right ones. In their old room, she'd have a record on, singing intermittently as she told Val what to expect, cosmically, for her future. There were a few ways to predict it: carved rune stones, a tarot deck, a necklace held above her hand. She'd fall in love, have three boys, and then a great calamity would befall her. The three boys troubled her more than the calamity.

Lily used her favorite necklace for that divination. The one Val had broken the clasp on, the necklace caught in Lily's hair at the nape while Val held her hair back as she wretched over the toilet at Meth Mouth Craig's. "This is so stupid," Val was telling her, although it wasn't what she meant exactly. "So *stupid*." And Lily, green at her cheeks with a wet red mouth, turning to look at her with eyes like holes. No, with burning eyes, the black primordial ferocity of a person willing to die, to kill; a creature steeped in death. But Lily had amber eyes, not black. These belonged to somebody else.

When she was sixteen, she'd gotten a black eye from a skinhead's elbow at her first and last mosh pit. People would always try to beat you down. You had to arrange your own protection.

Doug from the train, explaining how fertile Siberian soil would be, once they'd destroyed the rest of the world. "*They?* They don't give a *fuck*." She still had his cocaine.

This barrage was her mind's attempt to make disparate impressions cohere. It would draw in anything that might explain, through comparison or connection, what she'd seen in George the night before. None of it made any sense. He was great to his students. Even his enemies admitted that. Rave reviews from his undergraduate teaching evaluations, tenure track placements for his graduate advisees. And she wasn't just his advisee. There had been some sort of miscommunication. Something inexplicable reaching out from the cave, making him act against his nature.

She felt better near the afternoon, and Kit's discovery served as a good distraction. The four of them sat together in the cool air of the cave to discuss. They huddled like children, and she talked them all up into a daydream with her. "This is arguably the most important needle in the world, in human history," and so on. You could say anything was the most important in human history as long as you said "arguably" first. The boys loved it.

"Human or prehuman, pre-*sapiens*, that is," said Kit.

"Possibly," added Mark. They all nodded gravely, like serious people, before returning to the possibilities, the far-reaching implications.

At dinner they rehashed every possibility like children running inventory on their Halloween candy. Val shivered, though she wasn't cold. George touched her hand. Later, when Kit and Mark were asleep, she went to him. She had to do it. If she didn't seek him out that night, he'd know she was afraid of him, that she'd seen the strange fire in his eyes. And then he would be lost to her forever. They'd nod at each other in the hallways and meet perfunctorily. He'd write her a glowing recommendation letter after she graduated, copied from earlier glowing recommendations to other former students with a few specifics switched out. She might as well be dead to him. That was the core of it: she would go to him now, or she'd die.

⚘

He met her in a pleasant mood, unaware that she'd just almost died. She didn't want to ruin anything by explaining it. He ran his finger along the sunburn at the collar of her shirt, then sent her out with a cigarette, citing a need to finish writing down an idea for his next book. She met Kit as he left the garden shed. She was about to say, *I thought you were asleep*, but decided that sounded suspicious.

When he left, she returned to George, who insisted on cleaning and rewrapping the cut on her arm, though he did a poor job of it. "It's funny," said Val, "what people pick up through the course of their lives and what they miss."

"Because I took so long to type my notes? I've never been a quick typist. I like to think through my ideas as I put them down."

"You wrapped the gauze too tight. You're supposed to let the skin breathe."

He watched as she rewound the bandage. "A nasty scrape."

"It's not so bad."

"You're careless. I used to think you were put-together."

"A mistake you're not the first to make."

"But you've got guts. That makes up for it."

They kissed, deeply, without urgency. He undressed her in a slow, sentimental way, lingering on each button of her shirt. She could see he was in a sentimental mood. Or, more exactly, a sentimental mood was on him. Emotions never transformed or overtook George; they just lightly and temporarily tinted the essential form of his personality, like water poured over a rock. A person like Kit, for example, could fundamentally change from hour to hour. How Melissa could tolerate this was a mystery. Maybe he feared her enough to mitigate it. Or maybe she, so solid in herself, didn't mind having a shapeshifter for a husband.

George made love to her sentimentally, then told her about his honeymoon in Malta, where his family owned a house that had been built during the Crusades on a Roman foundation. He described a moonlit walk on the beach with his young wife, when hundreds of dead jellyfish washed up on the shore. One stung his bride's foot, and he carried her back to the spot in the sand where they'd left their shoes. He liked this memory, the visions of death and love and moonlight, the image of himself carrying his little birdlike wife to safety like a knight, an old hero of myth. But he didn't seem lost in reverie, about to crumble under the weight of yearning and regret. She wasn't worried that he'd start to cry and send her away or, worse still, suddenly embrace her and weep into her shoulder.

She liked that he didn't feel too much. A person needed a certain amount of empathy in order to anchor his principles, some pathos to give and receive love, but anything more than the requisite chipped away at his competence. "And what was the house like?" she asked, just to hear him talk.

"Hardly habitable, really. None of us ever use it. Before Elizabeth and I arrived, it had been rented out to some British family for eight months, and they left it in squalor. Juice stains on the rug, mashed potatoes and gummy bears shoved into every crevice—and old houses have a lot of crevices. I think the children must have made a game of hiding food around the house. We hired some extra women to clean before our arrival, and God knows they tried. But it wasn't important to me then."

"Did it have turrets, from the Crusades?"

"Turrets, no. But there was a spot, a stone at the base of the entryway, where men had carved their names, going back centuries. Some had dates, some not. The oldest was, I think, 1534, written out in Roman numerals too."

"That's beautiful. From your family?"

"We didn't have the house then, no. But my uncle put his name in. And then Liz and I did too."

She had been lying on her stomach, supported by her elbows, but she sat up at this. She thought of Victorian tourists carving their names into Egyptian temples and pyramids. "*You* carved your name?"

"Well, why not? It's our house now. And history is a living thing."

And an old house was not a sacred temple. But it still seemed wrong. Emphatically wrong.

He said, "Do you hear that?"

A long, thin howl broke through from outside.

"Wolves?" She phrased this as a question, although nothing else could have made the sound. It was not the lone, hollow howl of the wind, but something throaty, multitudinous. George nodded. Another howl, this one closer.

"They're hunting."

The sounds of the wolves grew nearer and more frantic, rising in pitch as more and more wolves joined. Whatever they had killed, its screams were drowned by the yips and cries and lunatic bays of the wolves as they tore it apart. George and Val listened to all this in tense silence. Val realized that she was afraid. After the initial wave of visceral dread passed, wonder at the strangeness of the fear washed over her, giving her surroundings an air of unreality. She had never had to fear an animal before.

"Were you worried they'd come?" George asked, when the wolves were finally silent, their bloodlust sated.

"Yes," she admitted. "But they don't . . . they wouldn't?"

He laughed. "Mark wouldn't leave his tent when the wolves were so close. Common sense, really. And Kit would rather be eaten alive than come here."

"I meant the wolves."

"Oh. They won't come here," he said, and did not elaborate. He lunged to kiss her neck, and she let him, and they laughed.

She woke up very early, and for the first time she did not wake up alone. George was lacing up his boots and didn't notice when she blinked her eyes open. He left before the fog of sleep had fully cleared. What was he doing, going into the forest each morning? She thought, for a moment, that she should follow him. But that was ridiculous. Who did that? He was going on a walk, that was it. Slink back to your tent and dress yourself for the day, eat your sad oatmeal, walk up to the cave. That would be the wise course of action.

She had never followed anyone before but had some idea what to do from movies. Linger back about twenty feet, at an angle, and duck into opportune alleys or, in her case, behind trees. She was light on her feet and walked quietly. Not infrequently, she would sneak up on people accidentally. Doing it on purpose, however, felt very different. But she laced up her boots, not giving herself the time to back down, and slipped out just as he disappeared into the trees.

Wherever he was going, he knew the way. Kit and Mark would walk out sometimes, but they always stuck to the river. Val never strayed far from camp except to bathe, easily imagining herself getting lost in the woods. But as she followed George, he led her confidently in no discernible direction through the trees. They reached close to the river, but then turned away from it again. This went on for some time. It might have been ten minutes or forty. She worried she'd lose his trail. The wolves would find her before Kit and Mark did. Those wolves. The horrible sounds of the animals sent a real, physical shiver down her spine when she thought of them. It also seemed possible that George had seen her already and was leading her down a false trail.

He stopped at a sun-dappled clearing in the pines and bent to study the ground. Val couldn't see anything in it at first, but then realized that a wavy pattern was faintly visible in the dirt and dried needles, as if somebody had taken a brush to cover their tracks. George photographed this and walked around it to unhook something tied to a tree. It was small and brown, some sort of hunting camera. She leaned forward to see, and a twig snapped beneath the pressure of her shifting foot. He spun around. The look on his face turned quickly from fear to surprise to, as he walked quickly toward her, the most sickening expression of anger that she'd ever seen disfigure a man's face.

Mark read *STALIN* at breakfast again. If you didn't flip to the back of the book for every endnote and glossary term, it became readable.

And he would finish it. George had finished it. Marcus Aurelius would have finished it. Stalin himself, well, he was occupied elsewhere. But Mark knew, definitely if esoterically, that this was a test of the will.

Kit joined him eventually, and they walked up to the cave together. George was already there, rechecking pit measurements recorded the day before. He was alone.

"Where's Valerie?" Mark asked.

"At camp."

"We didn't see her."

George shrugged. After a moment, Mark and Kit dropped their backpacks and began to take out their supplies. They lingered above their test pits, unsure whether to start. Kit sighed, took a swig of water, and said with an air of decision that he would go to check if Val was in her tent.

George nodded. "Mark, can I see your trowel? Mine's a WHS, but I seem to have ended up with a Marshalltown somehow."

Mark held up his trowel, which said MARK A. in Sharpied block letters. Kit shook his head in disgust and left.

As he started to work, Mark couldn't help but think back to the wolves. The frenzy of their cries as they went in for the kill. Val was so strange in her habits, and she didn't know anything about the wilderness. It was irresponsible to bring her here at all, really. It would be so *easy* for something to happen. But this was paranoia. A girl missing for twenty minutes was not necessarily devoured by wolves. And yet, how would it look? That Kit went to check on her while he stayed up here to scrape a trowel across dirt like he did for seven hours every day. Decisive action. He needed to learn to take decisive action. Stalin would. Not that Stalin was a perfect model of behavior in all fields. Obviously. But there was something to admire, wasn't there, about a man who could make swift decisions?

"She's not there," said Kit. Mark hadn't heard him return. The three men stood silently for a moment, looking at one another.

"There must be a protocol for this?" said Mark. He hated himself for the questioning lilt in his voice. They'd gone over safety precautions so many times in Toronto and even on the train. But what had they said again? Drink as much water as you possibly can. Stay in the shade. Don't panic.

"The satellite radio," said Kit.

George shook his head and kept shaking it long after he'd made his point. "That's a bit hasty."

"Well," said Kit. "Where could she be?"

"The river. Or camp."

"I *checked* camp. She's not there."

"You checked everywhere?"

"Yes. And I called out for her. She's not there."

"I'll check the river," said George, "and if she's not there, we'll wait half an hour, then radio for help. But I'm sure it won't come to that."

Kit let out an inexplicable laugh. Every noise and gesture seemed tense and disconnected to Mark. This was the moment of crisis. A man takes decisive action.

"I'll go with you," said Kit.

George nodded, displeased. "Mark, you wait here."

When they were gone, he scraped the bottom of the pit half-heartedly for a few minutes before climbing out. He sat in the dirt with *STALIN* and a red pen. This was actually a bearable chapter, heavily narrative, where Stalin—or Koba, as he was known then—and his Bolshevik battle squad executed a series of heists stealing not rubles but printing equipment. But Mark just stared at the page. Valerie could be hurt, somewhere out in the forest. She could be dead. Well, if she was dead, then she was dead. But if she was dying? If she'd tried to climb, for some reason—she would do something stupid like that—and had fallen? If she was lying in a pile of rocks with two broken legs while he sat here underlining passages in a book he didn't even like? He wouldn't have had the guts to steal a printing press from the czarist newspapers. He was weak.

And he'd lost his watch. He couldn't even go down to camp at a set time to make a call from the satellite radio, because he couldn't tell the time. Where was that fucker who'd cheated him out of his watch? He should have beaten the man. Taken his watch back with either intimidation or force. Maybe he should go down anyway, make an executive decision to call for help early. But that was stupid. And even if it wasn't stupid, he wouldn't. Not when George told him to wait here.

A gust of cool wind blew from the cave. He shivered. There were noises coming from the cave. A sort of dragging, scraping noise. Atmospheric pressure changes, probably. But did that make any sense? He had a flashlight. He could go check. It would be better than sitting around.

He had forgotten his own flashlight and had to look through Kit's bag and then George's before locating one. He took some pleasure in rooting through their bags. This was necessary. He was investigating. After finally finding one, he could only turn it on and spin around before he found himself shining it directly in Valerie's face.

She shielded her eyes with a red hand. Red with blood. The other hand held some sort of metal tool. Not a flashlight. Her shirt was torn at the shoulder, and all her clothing was covered in dirt. Dirt coated her arms, her hair, and seemed to hang in a cloud around her, suspended in the artificial light. Her face was dirty too, wet with sweat. Her eyes, with pupils dilated in the half dark, seemed not to be looking anywhere.

"Valerie," he said stupidly.

"Mark," she said. "It's so beautiful. I have to show you."

She had a cut on her temple along with the one on her hand. "I need you to see it," she kept saying. "I need you to see it."

She seemed half insane, and he thought it better not to upset her. If it came down to it, he could probably just pick her up and bring her back down, but his curiosity won out. What did she need him to see? What was so beautiful?

He insisted on leaving a note for George, a precaution that made Valerie laugh uncontrollably. This seemed to support the theory that she'd somehow gone insane, though when he looked down at his note, held down with a rock at the mouth of the cave, he did see the humor.

George—
V is ok. We are in cave. ↑
—M

Mark led the way, as he had the flashlight and was unwilling to relinquish it. He hit his head a number of times as the passage shrank and eventually settled into a stooped posture and a shuffling walk. Valerie normally would have cracked a joke, or at least given some sort of look, but now she didn't notice. An invisible string seemed to draw her forward, deeper and deeper into the dark of the cave.

"How did you get back here without a light?" he asked.

"I had one, but I left it back there. I felt along the wall to get back, which was stupid." She pointed at the cut on the side of her face.

After some unaccountable hesitation, he posed the most pressing and obvious question. "What's back there?"

She laughed again, which was not reassuring. As they neared the spot where the cave fell in on itself, Mark could see a faint light emanating from the rubble. A pang of fear possessed him. He wanted to turn back. But her pace quickened, and he couldn't let her stumble into the dark alone again. He pressed on. When they reached the avalanche, it became clear that the light was coming from the hole at the top. It was also clear that the hole they had barely been able to look through before had been enlarged. Rocks had been removed or pushed aside. He stubbed his toe on a football-sized cluster of debris he was sure hadn't been there anymore.

Val motioned up at it. "Here. Look in."

"What did you do?"

She gestured upward silently, and he stepped closer. Where she'd enlarged the hole she'd placed her headlamp upright in the center with a few small rocks stacked at the base so it didn't fall over in a subterranean breeze.

"You were *inside*?"

Val's flashlight was illuminating a small chamber about the size of a large bedroom. His eyes wandered upward, showing him what had moved Val so much, what she'd needed him to see.

The three black streaks they'd all glimpsed led upward toward the curved ceiling. They were legs, the long, graceful legs of animals running. They blurred together into an indistinct haze of limbs, a stampede, leading up into the strong overlapping bodies of deer, heads bobbing up, great antlers branching out from the blur of the crowd. The antlers were the only part of the image that seemed to stay still. The rest, even in the static light of the headlamp, danced across the pitted wall of the cave. Below them were more animals: lions, bears, aurochs, and bison moving outward to cover every surface of the cave, painted in black, in ocher, in vivid red, all of them moving, running, pausing in the light, skulking in the shadows. The room seemed to throb like a heart.

12

ANATOLIY ARRIVED THE NEXT MORNING TO BRING THEM BACK to Yakutsk for the weekend. They were all in rough shape: sunburned with uneven tans, their clothes stiff from soap they hadn't managed to fully wash out and hanging at angles off their thin frames—everybody always lost weight on a dig. And, of course, there was the smell.

"Indy!" he said to George, who apologized for the stench of two weeks in the woods. Anatoliy explained, as they boarded the aircraft, that he was unaffected, having lost his sense of smell to a severe fever in early childhood. "Mostly it is okay to not smell. Here it is good. But then there was petrol leak once."

Exhausted, nobody inquired further into this, and Anatoliy, who seemed starved for conversation, changed tack as soon as they had taken off and gained enough altitude to allow for a lower level of concentration. "Find any mummies?"

Kit looked out the window.

"Well, not exactly," said Val.

George made a quip in Russian, and Anatoliy laughed.

"Every time I ask, and every time George tell me how it is. Sharp rocks and old cave trash."

"We found a needle," said Val.

"Needle is . . ." He held out one of his palms flat and mimed sewing along it with the other.

"Yes!" she raised her voice in alarm, realizing he had neither hands nor eyes on the controls. He laughed, pretended to prick his flat hand with the imaginary needle, shook out the mimed wound with theatrical vigor, and turned back to adjust the yoke.

"What is so great about needle?"

"Its age. Well, its possible age. If it is what we think it is, nobody's ever found anything like it."

"Nobody has found needle? I go to house of grandmother; I find needle."

"It's possibly the earliest known example," attempted Mark.

"Can I borrow old needle? I have hole in my sock." He chuckled at his own joke. Nobody replied. They might have tried to defend their discovery, pointlessly and on principle, had they not all been so tired and so caught up in the daze of their other brilliant discovery. They felt, all of them, removed from time. The discovery was not a discovery made on the brink of the millennium, in the age of twenty-four-hour news and plastic cutlery. It was something out of the heroic age of archaeology—Schliemann blasting through nine layers of Troy with dynamite; Carter prying open the antechamber door to Tutankhamun's tomb, the ailing Earl of Carnarvon peering over his shoulder. These stories horrified all modern archaeologists, yet drew them in like accounts of illicit love affairs. Val wondered what they'd think of her climbing through the avalanche, risking a collapse inward onto the paintings. But of course, they didn't have to ever know about that.

Past her sheer wonder at the paintings' existence, Val couldn't quite believe their beauty. The paint looked so fresh in some areas of the chamber, where the calcium drips were less severe. Like they'd been touched up last week. Though she knew it was wrong, Val had put her hand on the wall when she'd first climbed through, tracing her fingertips along the soot-black flank of an aurochs, the whole expanse of human history crushed up between them like a soda can under the heel of a boot.

"In America, you have no need to sew holes. You buy new socks!"

"We're Canadian," said Mark.

Val sighed at nothing in particular. She was hardly there at all. She was still standing in the cave, touching the flank of the aurochs. "Well."

It was strange to see everybody turn into themselves again—into the versions of themselves, that is, that they usually inhabited—over the course of their first afternoon back in Yakutsk. Mark's transformation was the most obvious but, in some sense, the least complete. He was allowed (and silently compelled) to shower first, wiping away dirt and an empire of foul bacteria from his skin, shaving off the tufty red beard he'd let ferment over the course of the past two weeks. Still, he maintained his morose silence, fixating on his *STALIN* tome, fidgeting, sighing, humming "Greensleeves." At dinner, Val caught him staring at her scraped-up hands with an inexplicable, primal hate.

Kit, still edgy on the plane, regained his suave, elegant manners by the time they met up with Vasiliy. The shower did him good too. He'd kept up a rigorous standard of hygiene in the taiga, but with only the river to wash both body and clothes in, he'd begun to smell like it. This wasn't a bad smell, exactly, but an unexpected one to emanate from a person so close to earning his doctorate at a highly respected research university.

Val herself was startled by the changes paved roads and permanent shelters wrought on her psyche. She felt the weight of society, of the code of socially acceptable behavior, begin to bear down on her just from looking at its setting. She had not acted logically on the dig. Whether due to isolation, endless light, George, or some combination of the three, she'd gone half mad in the wilderness. She thought back to the train, joking with Kit about Mark snapping and killing somebody. "If anyone snaps," he'd said, "it'll be you."

Only George, with his perfect posture and his elegant gestures, expressing each passing thought in a full, grammatically correct sentence, remained unchanged. He was as lucid and coherent as ever in any setting, for any length of time. From a certain distance, his personality had the heft and solidity of steel. But she had sustained this illusion longer and more completely than George himself could have managed without her assistance.

She had needed him as a statue. She had made her grand sacrifice at its foot. Only afterward did she realize she hadn't done it to prove her devotion to George but to prove to herself that he was in fact what she needed him to be. That he was still a myth, an ideal, a marble pillar. Now she couldn't look at him. He kissed her and his face felt like a mask. A cheap, new rubber mask with a burning, writhing creature behind it, staring at her with embers through the eyeholes. Well. There was no obvious way to get out of it without making a scene, or at the very least a statement, so she kissed back. After all, she'd done it to herself. How stupid to kiss him that first night on Vasiliy's porch. How stupid to follow him through the woods that final morning.

He never addressed what he'd said to her out in the clearing, never even alluded to it. He was exactly the same as he'd always been: sophisticated, worldly, and, above all, coherent. That was the terrible thing. She now felt she could have loved him if he'd fallen apart afterward.

But then the thought of him crying repulsed her. Maybe she'd never loved him at all.

As things stood, she had another five weeks before they flew back to Canada, and there was no point in making any drastic move before that. She'd already been impulsive rushing into the thing; to pull out suddenly could ruin everything she'd been working toward. Would he cut her out from the story of the cave's discovery? Would he ruin her reputation, sabotage her thesis? A week ago, these thoughts would have seemed ridiculous. But now she knew how little she knew him. How little, maybe, it was possible to know a person in whom chaos and order were so distinctly partitioned.

All afternoon, she felt him watching her. She was freshly scrubbed, her hair still wet, and wearing her cleanest article of clothing, the black shift dress she'd worn to dinner in Moscow. (Dinner at Vasiliy's made the dress a more plausible option. Everybody dressed for dinner here, either because it was expected or because their nice clothes were the only fresh ones.) Her dress was still stained with that thick, bloodlike wine George had ordered for the table, when she'd gotten too drunk and told Mark he'd get hit by a taxi. Why did she always have to say such crazy things to people? The stain, in any case, was barely visible against the black fabric. She'd mostly dabbed it out with a napkin and some hand soap on the train.

George sat next to her on Vasiliy's couch, both of them silently reading (he, a book on early mapmaking and Cartesian geometry; she, a Victorian novel about orphans dying of consumption). He had something to say, she felt, but Vasiliy was writing a letter in the corner, and his presence stifled any real conversation. She knew, with preternatural certainty, that he would follow her outside if she went to smoke a cigarette, so she ignored the urge and volunteered to watch the baby as Tuskulaana went out to buy meat and vegetables.

"We have a girl to do it," said Vasiliy, not looking up from his work.

"No, I love kids!" She said this with more enthusiasm than she really felt, but she did like children, generally, for the same reason she liked talkative strangers: they had no standards for behavior. While she often couldn't help but upset acceptable people, and always held them at a distance, she could fall rapidly into a natural rapport with someone with no formed expectations like a stranger or a child.

She let the baby play with her north arrow, which he enjoyed, and engaged in a game where they stuck Post-it notes on each other's faces. He warmed very quickly to her and tried to follow when she left for the bathroom, babbling in a disjointed mix of Russian and Sakha. When she returned to the living room, both George and Vasiliy were gone. Little Vasya was engaged in pulling apart her Post-it pad. She took him with her and sat him on her lap under the dining table, projecting her flashlight onto the long, heavy tablecloth and making a series of shadow puppets George had taught her in a moment of whimsy. The baby very helpfully named the animals as she formed them: Krolik. Medved. Börö. It was there that Tuskulaana, arms full of paper bags, found them, tracing the sound of her son's voice from the front hall.

"Sorry . . ." said Val stupidly, but Tuskulaana seemed to like her better after this. She gave her a genuine smile as she gathered up her child.

With nothing to do, Val decided to run up Vasiliy's phone bill. She sat in the kitchen, calculating the time difference and trying to figure out who in Toronto might be up at six in the morning, then decided to call Lily instead.

Defying her conscious judgment, her fingers dialed +1 for the United States and then her sister's 818 phone number. Talking to Lily was an exhilarating experience that always left her feeling disoriented and faintly unclean. Afterward, she'd try to regain a sense of reality by handling practical tasks like washing dishes or filling out paperwork, but the room around her would persist in feeling like a plastic diorama for hours. This was not only because Lily was her sister and they naturally had a long, complicated history, not because Val had spent years of her youth judging herself only in relation to Lily. It was just a quality of Lily's personality, a way she had of submerging whomever she met into a warm bath of energy, then talking to her own reflection above the face of her helpless, hypnotized victim until they stopped struggling. In another sense, she was wonderful. She picked up on the first ring.

"Marcel?"

"No."

"Vallie! How are you?"

"Who's Marcel?"

"Just some whatever. But you're in Russia! That must be wild. Is it cold?"

"No, it's hot. There are a bunch of mosquitoes even."

"Huh, weird."

They went through a few formalities before Val attempted to disclose her reason for calling with a neutral "Can I ask you something?"

"Yeah, go ahead. You know I had a premonition you'd call and say something like that."

"It's about George," she persisted.

"He's the professor? The left-handed one?"

This prompted a pang of affection. Only Lily would have retained this detail, to the exclusion of all relevant information. "Yeah."

"Never trust a left-handed man. It means he had a twin in the womb and he absorbed it. So he's split, he's two people. You know, Gemini. Or he's kind of like an adult man carrying the ghost of a baby inside him. It's sad. They're marked by death."

"I mean, I'm not sure. I don't think all left-handed people ate their twins, though."

"So ask if he has a twin, and if he says no, you know where it went."

"Oh."

"All their organs are reversed in their bodies. It makes them unbalanced. Jimmy's left-handed. But then he's a very passionate, childlike person."

Jimmy was a Hollywood stunt double who'd given Lily chlamydia the previous winter. Val was alarmed to hear her speak of him in the present tense.

"I know he's crazy," said Lily, before Val could comment. "He keeps saying civilization is gonna crumble in the year 2000. All the electronics and computer systems will short-circuit, and we'll be plunged into a new age of darkness."

"Yikes."

"He wants me to move to Wyoming with him to live off the land. But I don't think he's for real. I mean, he's so bad with commitment. One second it's 'I don't want anything serious,' and then it's 'I'm gonna teach you how to hunt.' I dunno."

"Probably still on coke."

"Oh, he is."

"Go with Marcel instead."

"Marcel is nobody. A business connection."

Val never got around to asking about George. She could have told her sister everything, and she wouldn't have judged her. George had sworn them all to secrecy on the subject of the cave, but this wasn't a real concern for Val. While Lily was not discreet, nobody she knew would care about an archaeological discovery, and even if she managed to find some lost academic huddled in a doorway at a Beverly Hills house party, nobody ever believed anything she told them.

But beyond that, Val found she couldn't talk about George. She couldn't possibly explain what he'd done, or what she'd done, or, most obscure of all, *why*. Easier, then, to advise on Chlamydia Jimmy.

They ended their call, as they often did, with Lily telling Val to come visit her in California and Val promising she'd do so. Lily had lived in Los Angeles for seven years. Both women knew by now that Val would never actually visit her there, but there is comfort in a ritual.

13

Val sat alone in a clean, underfurnished café. It had the distinct look of a repurposed office building, with a dropped fiberboard ceiling and coarse gray carpet. A teenager played *Tetris* on an arcade machine in a corner, and about a dozen others gathered around him, waiting for their turn. Otherwise, there were no customers.

George had taken her into town for supplies. They'd replenished the first aid kit and bought more sad camp food, extra film for their cameras, cheap yellow paper, nicer bleached cotton paper, a spare typewriter ribbon. He radiated satisfaction the whole time, not daring to speak of the cave in public but alluding to it with little inward smiles, meaningful looks to Val. There was no drastic alteration, only a slightly easier way of speaking, a readier laugh. No evidence proved him any less composed than he normally was. She'd tried to smile back, to match his energy, but she found herself unable to respond naturally to anything he said.

Then he'd left her in a nearby park to run an unspecified errand. Though the gnats were out in swarms, she predominantly felt relieved by this development.

She'd sought shelter in the café, chosen because it overlooked the park. It wasn't air-conditioned but did have some natural insulation and fewer gnats. She positioned herself at a table facing the glass storefront so she could watch for George's return. She had a book to read and a shopping list to review, both placed on the table to indicate some sense of purpose. She didn't try to read them, though. A hazy, unfocused feeling had enveloped her.

The *Tetris* player groaned, and the machine played a mocking "game over" tone. Another teenager laughed, and a silent third took the loser's spot. The proprietor of the café saw her looking as he brought her coffee and informed her in slow, kindly Russian that they would soon be selling the *Tetris* machine to replace it with *Mortal Kombat*, or something else to do with *Mortal Kombat*, which he referred to by its English title, or possibly something to do with actual mortal combat, though this seemed unlikely.

The front bell rang and the door swung open. The proprietor turned to greet the new customer, but instead the man walked straight up to Val. She was too surprised, for a moment, to recognize him, but his identity hit her as the smell did: cheap vodka, sweat, tobacco. A fleshy pink person, he was wearing a new suit of cobalt polyester. "Doug?"

"Lady Di! Thought I'd see you around at some point."

"You did?"

"C'mon. I waved to you at the station. You were ignoring me."

"I didn't see you."

"Felt kinda used. You just kept walking. Not even a smile." He examined her. She knew she looked exhausted, slightly disheveled. "But you're not a smiler, are you?"

She smiled with closed lips. "I really didn't see you. I didn't think you were getting off here."

George was due to return soon, and she didn't want to have to explain Doug to him. The American had a slightly crazed look in his eye, and she worried he might follow her out to the park. The proprietor tapped his shoulder and handed him a Russian menu. Doug, still lurking by Val's table, laughed and handed it back.

"Coffee?" asked the proprietor.

Doug gave him a yellow-nailed thumbs-up. He leaned over Val's table after the man left, reading her shopping list aloud. "'Bandages, quinine, coffee powder, film roll'—this a code or something?"

"Yeah."

He held it at a distance, squinted with vaudevillian flair. "I figured. Find anything good in the cave?"

Val paused for a moment. "Not really."

"Great news for me, you know. Sometimes when there's something buried out in the woods, they won't let you develop. Cultural heritage." He spoke these last words with exaggerated disdain, gathering energy. She nodded, and her fatigue seemed to excite him further. He laughed again, a little too loudly. "Now, we're getting in at a good time, mind you—a new government, very agreeable and reasonable and whatnot. I've got guys, Russians. My boys Vasiliy and Igor who have friends who have friends—that's how it all comes together."

"Vasiliy who?"

"Business associate. That's the key to this whole thing—to business, to everything—getting in at the right time. And that's how you make history instead of digging it up. No offense, honey. I'm glad you didn't find anything, anyway."

Val recoiled at the epithet "honey," which Doug noticed and ignored. He had been amusing in his way on the train, but his presence felt wrong here and unpleasantly significant. He was too incoherent to be a messenger, exactly. More like a harbinger. Was it a kind of test?

Strange coincidences darting around each other, so close to connecting. But you could make anything connect—something she'd learned in the social sciences, reading some of the more far-fetched papers produced by her teachers and peers—and it still didn't mean very much.

Having lingered long enough without an invitation, Doug pulled out the chair opposite hers and sat down. "I knew we'd see each other again. Call it fate. I have a keen eye for fate. Or you could say it's business intuition."

Val gathered her energy and stood up. "Doug, it was nice to see you, but I have to go meet my colleague."

"Oh, don't be like that. Was it the history stuff? I'm just joking around!"

After paying, she walked quickly through the park, feeling his eyes on her from the café, then slipped into a shop for candy and cigarettes.

Later, in the afternoon, Vasiliy's chauffeur took Mark into town to buy a watch and a new sleeping bag. When he got there, though, Mark found himself incapable of entering any shops. Attempting an interaction in Russian felt impossible. Months ago, he'd bought himself a set of Govori Po-Russki! tapes for Christmas and had achieved an impressive level of conversational Russian in the interim. He'd practiced on the train too, although he'd been too shy to strike up conversations, instead settling for eavesdropping in the dining car and asking waiters if they rejected the weather. But now the thought of fumbling through numbers with a snide shopkeeper filled him with such a preemptive mix of base dread and acidic indignation that he had no idea what he might do if forced to engage with another living being.

Instead he just walked, slowly, in a deliberate plod. The city ran past him like a strip of film, its wide streets getting dirtier the farther he walked from the city center, its freshly paved roads already cracking, its Lego-block buildings and oversized statues of great dead men giving the sense of a metropolis designed to be empty, shut up for long winters of subsistence. But, against nature, every Siberian in the republic seemed to be out on the streets of Yakutsk that hot afternoon: Yakutians lounging on benches, at creaky tables outside cafés, on blankets in the park, laughing, flirting, arguing politics, ignoring vicious gnats. Some scrawny cigarette-smoking teenagers, sitting on the sidewalk, broke out into wild laughter. They were looking at him, he felt sure.

He was supposed to meet the car again by a statue of a Cossack with an axe at exactly half past six. Having no idea how long he'd been walking, he needed to actually buy a watch in order to achieve that feat. This fact would normally compel him to action. Today it seemed a remote concern. What did any of this matter?

He felt certain that the endless hours of light in Siberia were encroaching on his sanity as they never had in Alaska. After the discovery of the paintings, he had treated himself to some selections of Lovecraft, which he'd been saving. This was a mistake, the human psyche being as permeable as it was. Reality grew more tenuous under the writer's influence.

But at least it made his problems less personal. It was the existential question, on a grand scale, that had really been giving him trouble. We were all simply animals who had stumbled accidentally into this extra dimension of conscious thought, and it was an inherently confused, painful, lonely state. That was all.

For two nights in a row, Mark had dreamed an identical dream about the three of them—George, Valerie, Kit—sitting on the rocks at the mouth of the cave. They sat very still and close together, though not touching, all three with their ink-black hair, black eyes, unsmiling mouths, and colorless clothes of serious people. Against the pale morning sky, they could have been in a black-and-white photograph. A group pose, a family set—he himself against them, positioned as the photographer, but with no camera to justify his presence.

Then George's skin seemed to regain its olive color, and his eyes deepened with a strange burning quality. He would open his mouth to speak, to say something very important, but Valerie would interrupt him with a malicious giggle.

Mark was lonely. He'd always been lonely. Once, he'd thought this was a temporary state. He'd get out of Alaska and find people like himself. But there were no people like him. Maybe nobody was like anybody. Not to say they were all interesting or special, only that they were all very alone, their souls very specifically deformed. He felt a stab of bitterness and turned sharply to the left at the end of the block to indulge it.

But why bother with all this internal whining? Because a girl didn't like him? A girl whom he didn't like either, most of the time, even if he did love her. Well, there it was. He loved her. And the overwhelming force and stupidity of this love, undeniable once acknowledged, made him laugh out loud. This earned a few glances on the street.

When he first met her, he'd been ardent and sincere in his affection. He had liked her sleepy smiles in their eight a.m. class, her willingness to disagree. He'd bought a new shirt for their date and called ahead to reserve a table at an Italian restaurant. He did all this before asking her to dinner, feeling his courage would fail him otherwise. Not that he'd expected her to accept him. She seemed ethereal then, belonging to another plane of existence—how could she even consider him?

Then, in the middle of the restaurant, she took out a cigarette. He looked at her in dismay, and she offered him one.

"Those things are really bad for you, you know."

"Well. Fingers crossed." She turned back to her menu. He knew he ought to let it go.

"I mean, have you actually seen the statistics?"

"I only smoke about three a week," she said. "It's really fine."

"I just think, for people in the sciences, it doesn't make sense—"

"Do you think of what we do as science?"

"Of course!"

She lit her cigarette. "It just seems like sort of an arbitrary designation, in my opinion."

"We employ the scientific method."

"Well, sometimes. But you have to agree it doesn't have the same parameters as, say, physics. As the hard sciences, I mean. And I don't think we need to dress up as a hard science to be important. It's like lowering yourself, then asking for permission to matter, you know? And besides, that sort of outlook can make you inflexible."

"There is no such thing," he said stiffly, "as a *hard* science or a *soft* science."

From there, they disagreed on everything from recreational drug use to the human capacity for free will to *Star Wars* ("I like the gay robots, but otherwise it's kind of boring"). Their waiter came over frequently to refill their glasses, listening in with sadistic amusement. It was the most contentious date he'd been on in his life. At the end of it, though, he insisted on walking her back to her apartment, and they parted with only a nod. Neither suggested that they do this again sometime.

He went to sleep satisfied, having gotten in some pretty good points and won most of their arguments. That would have been the end of it, but when he woke up the next morning, he found himself more in love than ever. He thought maybe they could have that sort of rapport where you argue all the time without really meaning it. People had arrangements like that. When he saw her next, though, outside of class, talking to George, she greeted him coldly.

For years, their relationship consisted of constant, low-level conflict. This felt bearable. There was a wonderful tradition of friendship blossoming in just such a way. And maybe more. But now she rarely noticed him even to contradict him. Her head was full of something else. Full of George. That was the worst of it. She'd castrated him and cut him off from George in a single swipe of the blade.

Mark's love for George had been arguably greater than his love for Valerie. It had a more practical basis, at any rate. His father, though probably still alive, had contributed nothing more to Mark's life than the convenience of a Canadian passport to stash alongside his American one. He had a stepfather, Gary, who spat dip into old Spam cans and filled Mark's mother's house with three little half siblings whose dishwater hair and sledgehammer souls resembled Gary's so exactly that Mark could never really love them.

George was the first example he'd seen of a man who led a life both active and intellectual. He had openly sought his approval—showing up to office hours twice a week just to talk shop, reading every book George lent him in a week or less—and won it. George saw Mark as he wanted to be seen. He trusted him. He made a point of taking him aside to consult him. By now, halfway through Mark's degree, he was already talking about the positions he'd help him get at various universities across Canada, the United States, and even Europe.

But to see his hand laid so casually on her shoulder. To see him then look away when she tried to meet his eye. To see her stumble out from the dark, caked in dust and half mad from visions of the past. "Val's always been sort of stupid about things like this. About risks, I mean," Kit had told him drunkenly the night before. "But I never thought she'd be so stupid as to risk her life."

He cast them in different roles in his head. George as ruthless, experienced seductor; Val as a waiting daisy, plucked by a careless hand. Val as femme fatale, blowing smoke like a cynical actress, bedroom eyes hard as flint in the daylight; George as hapless, distracted intellectual, finding himself quite suddenly writhing in her web. Both of these scenarios were more appealing than what he felt was essentially the truth: that the people he'd held up as heroic archetypes for years were now involved in a base, squalid affair, creeping through shadows to paw at sweaty flesh. And he was their captive audience.

He also felt that in some sense, his presence was erotic to them. The fact that he may or may not realize added a thrill of collusion. Without it, they'd be left to stew in their own personalities. In a way, he made the whole thing possible. That was the most sickening aspect.

It seemed natural that a discovery as miraculous as the painted cave would eclipse Mark's misery and reveal the triviality of its source in the face of eternity. And when he first saw the deer and the lions winding around the cave wall, black as wet ink and red as fresh blood after unknown millennia, it did. But with a few days and a few hundred miles distance, this sense of obliterating awe began to fade, leaving in its place a pervasive sense of unreality and a new angle from which to reproach himself—after all, they'd just made one of the most significant archaeological discoveries in history, and all he could think about were petty interpersonal concerns. He tried to imagine himself sharing news of the cave when he got home and realized he had no one to tell.

It was this thought that absorbed him when he saw Klaus Kinski look back at him, then duck into the church across the street. Those sunken eyes, that unmistakable Neanderthal's jaw. Not the real Kinski, of course, but the man from the train. The bastard who'd stolen his watch.

The man probably still had it wrapped around his grubby wrist. How would he react if Mark walked up from behind, tapped him on the back, and demanded his property? Most people would be too surprised to do anything but comply. But if worse came to worst, he could beat him in a fight. He was larger, younger, and, suddenly, filled with righteous fury. He'd been cheated. He had an opportunity to strike back. And if Kinski thought he could hide behind God, he was mistaken. Nothing mattered much to him then. So why not beat a man into the floor of a church?

With this idea, he crossed the street and pushed through the heavy doors of the church. It didn't look very old, as churches went, with a gray plaster exterior and undersized square windows. The building could have passed for an office, if not for the small cross-topped blue dome attached to the roof. There was a larger, nicer cathedral painted peach with gilded spires somewhere in the city—Mark had seen it when he'd first arrived in Yakutsk. The streets around that church were cleaner. He'd been walking for what felt like hours and must have wandered into a part of the city with lower standards for holiness.

Inside was a dozen rows of fresh pine pews, recently cut and poorly varnished. A few old Russian women, wrapped in layers of dark cloth despite the heat, sat far apart on the pews, one of them whispering something to herself, another rocking slightly. They all faced toward a carving of an emaciated greenish Jesus on the cross, backlit with a heavenly electric glow. No Kinski.

Mark became aware, slowly, that the place was not silent. A noise like pebbles falling to the ground sounded from the left, where a single workman—middle-aged, paunchy, and jaundiced from drink—stood with a chisel, chipping plaster from the westward-facing wall of the church. The plaster came off in small chunks and fell through a dusty cloud like a shower of miniature meteors. Light from the small windows streamed in to illuminate the suspended dust and, through it, the image the workman was uncovering. The fresco, though less than half revealed, was striking in its beauty. Mark had no store of knowledge to pull from in order to date a Eurasian religious fresco, but the work gave off the impression of being very old and made him question his earlier assumption that the church had been newly built.

There were angels, a whole swarm of them, descending from Heaven. And not fat little cherubs either, but grown men with long, fiery wings and focused eyes, flat overlapping halos surrounding their heads. The angel at the head of the band was larger than the others, his face more vividly painted. He reached down to touch a man, who looked up at him with the most despairing expression.

If he'd ever been there at all, Klaus Kinski was gone now. But the church had broken through Mark's fatalistic mania, and he left it calmly after a few somber minutes standing near the door, watching the workman uncovering angels, the women praying, the backlit prophet draped seductively against his bloody cross. He traced his way back to the statue of the Cossack easily, though he hadn't been paying much attention to his route. This gave some small satisfaction. Mark had a natural sense of direction and, in fact, was blessed with an aptitude for most practical tasks, though he had no genius, and Valerie Howe would never love him. He could think about such things now as if they were traits and circumstances belonging to a stranger.

But then he saw him again. Kinski, slipping around a corner. He was only a block ahead, his filthy trench coat tucked under one arm, its tail grazing the pavement each time he lurched forward, and a leather briefcase in the opposite hand. There was nobody else on the street. They were alone. Without thinking, Mark pursued.

The older man heard his pounding footsteps as he approached and turned. He was too startled, when he saw Mark hurtling toward him, to do anything but stand and wait for him. Mark grabbed him by the collar. The material of his shirt had been worn so thin it nearly tore. He looked older than Mark had remembered, less vital. The lines in his face were white from uneven blood flow, and a peeling sunburn ran across his nose. He put up no resistance. Mark felt a little like a pet dog who, after years of trying, had finally caught a rat and now had no idea what to do with it.

He looked down at Kinski's hands to see if he was going for a knife, but both now clutched the briefcase.

"My watch," said Mark.

The man did not reply. Mark released his collar but did not step back. His bewilderment ebbed, replaced again by indignation. He held his wrist in front of Kinski's face and tapped it.

"Vremya," he said.

The man nodded and slowly lowered himself until he was squatting on the pavement, briefcase placed carefully in front of him. He opened it to reveal a tangled heap of watches. Mark kneeled on the other side and began to sift through the mess. He picked out the Timex easily but found its digital screen cracked and blinking.

He grabbed it up anyway, nodded at the man, and left.

14

After dinner, Vasiliy brought out a box of Cuban cigars, a gift, he explained, from his father upon the birth of his son. "They're harder to find now, but he has a whole closet full of them at home. He waited until Vasya was born to send them." He laughed, handing one cigar to George and another to Kit. Kit thought briefly of his own closet full of birdhouses. How different it would be to have a father who gave cigars. By then, Val and Tuskulaana had drifted off to the kitchen, Mark to his bed to read.

"Why did he wait?"

Vasiliy looked at Kit with gentle amusement. "Wanted to make sure it was a boy."

"What would he have given for a girl?" asked George.

Vasiliy thought for a moment. "Nothing. Or money."

"I have a little boy, about seven months younger than yours," said Kit. He'd developed a talent, since the birth of his baby, for estimating the ages of small children down to the month.

Vasiliy nodded approvingly, handing a pack of matches to George, who smelled his cigar before he lit it. "A boy is good. For the family, you know."

George handed the matches to Kit, who smiled at him as he took them. A funny thing had happened. At the same time as his judgments toward George solidified, his feelings toward him softened. Kit noticed this change in himself and tried to justify it in a number of ways. First, it was easier to appreciate a man's good qualities once his bad ones were clearly defined. By preparing for another person's faults, you can mitigate them and let their advantages shine through. And besides the business with Val, what had George really done wrong? He felt more frustrated with Val throughout the weeks of the dig and less accountable to her as a friend. She had made her choices.

These justifications, though, were only a small part of the change. Mostly, he felt a renewed liking for George because George had brought him to the cave and made his career. This reason, though tangibly beneficial, made him feel petty and selfish. He tried to brush it aside.

"I don't want any," said George. "Boys or girls. They take too much time."

"You might have one already, in Mongolia or Buryatia."

George laughed, and Kit, though the unsmiling image of his wife's face flashed through his mind, laughed too. George blew out a long snake of smoke and gave Kit a knowing look. He knew what this look referenced and would normally have resented it.

Once, at a faculty Christmas party, Kit had kissed another woman. Min-Seo, pregnant with David, had accompanied him but left when the drunks began to bicker. Kit had quarreled with George, and Min had gone to the bathroom, then told him to take a taxi home if he insisted on harming his career further. He'd stayed behind, by then absorbed in a conversation about Cortes's methodical destruction of Aztec codices with a German girl who had just submitted a thesis on Mesoamerican bookbinding. Her name was Lisa Schlesing, and she was very pretty in a high-cheeked, dark-eyed, serious way. Val said she looked like Tess of the d'Urbervilles.

They were talking very sentimentally about lost knowledge in the hallway outside the rec room, when they suddenly found themselves alone, in a spell of heavy silence. Impulsively, rather drunk, he'd brushed a lock of blond hair from her face. Lisa kissed him, and he kissed back for just a moment. This was long enough, however, for the department chair to peek in and draw his own conclusions and share them.

From this, Kit had developed the reputation of a lothario within the department. If not for the possible repercussions, he would have found it funny. He'd only ever slept with three women in his life. He had heard rumors of his low character from Val (who, to her credit, had disbelieved the story so completely that she'd laughed as she related it back to him). George later attempted an oblique joke about the situation: "Our man of mystery—where does he go? And with whom?" in front of a few undergrads in his TA section. Kit had turned defensive, and they'd argued.

The possibility of it getting back to Min-Seo in either its genuine or its exaggerated form was slight but not negligible. She never gossiped, but had an unnerving way of knowing things despite this, and had recently floated the idea of hosting a dinner party for Kit's colleagues.

Besides this plan, which stemmed more from propriety than real interest, she'd been cold to him for months now. It seemed a strange tack to take with Kit, who could maintain a Cold War indefinitely with anyone from his thesis adviser to his father, but by the time he left for Russia, Kit had spontaneously bought her flowers four times. They had done very little, but maybe one of Vasiliy's diamonds would work better. She could likely see more of herself in a hard, shining stone than in the rotting vegetable matter of a bouquet.

Vasiliy poured a round of vodka, while George entertained himself with thoughts of his hypothetical bastards. "I could have five," he mused. "I wonder what they'd do in the world."

"Five little Georges," said Vasiliy.

"God only knows what havoc they'll wreak."

Though sworn to secrecy, he was tempted to tell Min-Seo about the cave. She couldn't be mad at him for leaving if he'd made history, after all. But then the paranoid thought occurred to him that the phones might be tapped, that the Russians would swoop in and steal their find out from under them. Vasiliy, though charming on a personal level, was exactly the sort of person who would have his phones tapped. He spoke of the KGB with a rancor that felt personal. And though the Soviet Union had collapsed externally, there was no reason to suppose their extensive surveillance network disbanded upon the announcement. The idea that Russian spies would interfere with an archaeological discovery, groundbreaking though it was, seemed too ridiculous to voice, but just convincing enough to keep him cautious on the phone and indoors generally. He'd tell Min about his needle. This had elated him every time he thought of it before the discovery of the painted chamber made it look insignificant.

She picked up on the second ring when he called, which he hadn't expected.

"I'm on rotation in an hour."

"Oh. Should I call tomorrow?"

"Tomorrow's no good. But you can talk to my mom if you want updates on David. Actually, could you talk to your mother for me? I want to know how old you were when you first sat upright. David's been hitting his milestones until now, but he's not sitting well. I wonder if it comes from your side? I know you had trouble with gross motor skills as a child."

"I was fine. I played baseball."

There was a short silence.

"Still, I'd appreciate it if you asked her."

Kit's mother, who consistently got her only son's age wrong by up to three years, could never provide this information, and Min-Seo knew it. He was about to say this to her, but instead he surprised himself with a plea: "Don't be hard on him."

"I'm not criticizing. I'm concerned."

"Well, don't be. He's a great baby. I mean, you can tell he's smart. He's very expressive."

"It's a question of balance, not expressiveness or general intelligence."

"He doesn't need balance. It's synonymous with mediocrity." Kit cringed internally after saying this. He sounded like George.

She sighed. "There's no point in talking about this with you when you're not here."

"I don't know, Minnie. This isn't the conversation I meant to have. How did we get on this?"

She paused before replying, then spoke in a grave, deliberate tone, as if she'd rehearsed the words. And maybe she had—she was never usually one for melodrama or philosophical generalizations. "I fell in love with you," she said, "because I thought I didn't have to explain these things to you."

After this, he called his parents, not expecting them to pick up either, so that he could say, a month from now, that he had tried to call. Unhappily, his father answered.

"Hi, Dad."

"Kit. You're home?"

"No. Still in Russia."

"This call must cost a lot."

"Yeah."

"What do you want then?"

"Nothing." He said this rather sharply, and his father didn't respond. "How are you?" he continued.

"Good. Your mother has been learning watercolor. We're getting jays this summer. They prefer the bamboo to harder woods, but it gets dents."

"That's good."

"It's data."

"Is Mom there?"

"No."

He paused a moment before pushing forward. "Do you remember when I was a baby, how old I was when I sat up? How many months?"

"No."

"Okay."

"You were normal."

"Well. I'll see you soon."

George, in his way, had figured out how to navigate life, but only by amputating whatever secret part of a person was needed to connect to other people. Vasiliy, though, had learned a way to live. He had money, a career, a connection to his land, and a family. A simple family, with a sweet little wife. Kit tried to imagine himself married to somebody like Vasiliy's wife and found himself repulsed. He hadn't wanted a marriage like his parents'. He hadn't wanted a woman he could subdue. He wanted his own wife.

He recalled, suddenly, an inspirational memoir he'd read, a baffling gift from his mother some months back. It had been written by a man who'd had a large part of his brain removed in emergency surgery after a paragliding accident. He'd survived against all odds but had lost the ability to speak his native language (retaining only the English he'd learned for his stockbroking career) and could no longer perceive depth or clearly remember any events occurring more than forty-five minutes in the past. He read a book of Buddhist maxims every morning and shifted his investment focus from stocks to real estate. "There is a strange sort of peace in my life after the accident," he wrote. "After all, is there any animal more serene than the common goldfish?"

He would buy a diamond for Min-Seo. He'd go to Vasiliy's office, where he often went after dinner, and ask him that night if he was still awake. He could picture him pulling out a tray of them from a drawer in his desk, though he knew this was silly.

Vasiliy's office door was thin and he could hear them talking through it. Their voices were muffled but discernible. At first, he thought only of how carelessly built the house was. His father's office had a heavy cherrywood door that opened with a loud click and closed with a thud. He could have killed somebody behind it and Kit would never have heard. That's how an office door should be, he felt, and Vasiliy seemed like a person who might care about that sort of detail. But the decor in his incongruous home looked haphazard enough to prove that he wasn't, and the door was only a hollow, whitewashed gesture toward the concept of privacy.

He didn't mean to listen in, but they sounded so serious. It seemed impossible to interrupt. And while they hadn't heard him walking up, they could easily hear him walk away. The sudden sound of his footsteps leading from the door would tell a tale of espionage, even if he was completely innocent. So he stayed and became less innocent.

Vasiliy spoke in a low, clipped tone, and Kit could make out none of it. George spoke louder and more clearly. "They come from the hills. They'll go back up. You'll never see them coming." He kept refuting some point of Vasiliy's. Kit couldn't make out the content of the argument, but he could tell it was contentious. "The price of land is not the issue," George said. "People will see the importance."

After Vasiliy spoke again, George responded sharply, "You're trying to keep them for yourself."

The Russian launched into a long, low response. Kit considered, for a moment, pressing his ear to the door, then turned to leave, trying to make his footsteps light. His first step was silent, but on his second he landed on a creaky board. The sound cut through the air like a splinter, and immediately George and Vasiliy fell silent.

Though Vasiliy's house looked large enough to give them separate spaces, Kit and Mark had been placed in a room together with twin beds set on opposite walls. Along with depriving Kit of solitude, this arrangement felt infantilizing. A summer camp at the end of the earth. Mark, still in jeans, was lying on top of the covers on his bed, reading *STALIN.*

Kit sat down to write a letter to Min-Seo at the room's sole desk, a surprisingly beautiful pinewood antique that fit into the disjointed luxury of the house about as well as anything else. Once he'd set up his supplies, though, he cleared his throat and turned to Mark. "Have you ever thought it was strange, the fact that we're staying in this house? And not a hotel or something?"

Mark looked up, startled. He'd hardly processed Kit's entrance. "No. I don't know. Why?"

"Because a grant should include funding for board. It's standard."

Mark looked at him a second, then looked back at his book. "I guess you could ask."

Kit sat a long time without writing, then rapidly composed a sweet and friendly message that could have been written by anyone to anyone. He needed a cigarette. "Have you seen Val?"

Mark shook his head, and Kit wandered away, finding Val's door open a crack. She was lying still on her cot as if dead in the dark, windowless room. It was rather late, he realized.

"What?" she asked, without a trace of sleep in her voice. She shifted slightly but didn't sit up.

"Nothing."

Back in the dining room, alone, he poured himself a glass of vodka. He'd had to open Vasiliy's liquor cabinet for it but felt that his choosing the mostly empty bottle they'd been drinking from at dinner mitigated the imposition. He disliked vodka and there was a nice, unopened bottle of cognac beside it on the shelf, but there were limits. He sat at the head of the table, in Vasiliy's chair, and swallowed without relish.

He returned to his room, tore up and rewrote his letter by the light of the desk lamp while Mark groaned in his sleep, then drifted back to the dining room. There he found Val, looking through the liquor cabinet. She selected the cognac, then turned around.

"Hey," she said, not very warmly. When they'd quarreled in the past, she would always be the first to make peace.

"Glasses on the top shelf."

She shrugged. "I was just going to drink from the bottle."

He got two glasses down, realizing as he did so that she probably couldn't reach that high. He pulled out a chair to sit down at the table.

"I'm going out to the porch," she said. "I don't like this room."

He followed her, and she handed him a cigarette out on the steps. She'd bought new ones in town, a whole carton of them. He examined the cigarette with mild suspicion.

"I made sure they were expensive," said Val, breathing out smoke and passing him a lighter. She took a joyless swig of cognac. This was a drink meant to be savored, but thinking back to the unnerving scene he'd heard in Vasiliy's office, he felt some sick pleasure in watching her down it like a high schooler. They said nothing for half a cigarette. This was a competitive silence, Kit realized. Still, he cracked first.

"I have a headache." He didn't really have a headache, and his motivation for this pointless lie was obscure even to himself.

"Oh. That sucks." There was no real commiseration in her tone, where usually there would be. He felt slightly offended on behalf of his fictitious ailment.

"Yeah."

"How's Melissa?"

"She's fine. At the hospital right now."

"And the baby?"

"He's good. I mean, he's a baby. She says he's not balancing as well as he should be by now. But I think it's nothing."

"It's so weird you have a kid."

They lapsed back into silence, drinking and smoking with grim, futile efficiency, like soldiers on the last night of leave.

"What do you think is wrong with Mark?"

Kit had wondered the same thing and came to the conclusion that he was having some sort of existential crisis. He'd tried to tell him some strange story about following a thief into a church before dinner, then gotten embarrassed and changed the subject halfway through. "I think it's the light."

"Yeah."

"It's getting to me too."

She laughed. "I've been miserable. Can't sleep more than four and a half hours a night, even with a mask. It's like I know it's there somehow."

"God."

"But it must be the sleep thing. I've been feeling ridiculous, you know, for being so miserable, and then that's only made me more miserable. The feeling ridiculous, I mean. After all, if you consider what we found . . ."

He poured them each another glass. "It's amazing."

She nodded.

"And in terms of our careers," he continued, after a moment. "I mean, Christ—in terms of everything we know about the origins of civilization."

"You sound like George." It was not these words but the way she said them that made him hesitate. She was, as far as he knew, devoted to George, but her voice had an edge to it. They talked around the point for a while. Kit remembered why he liked Val again, and she seemed to remember why she liked him. But he wasn't sure he could trust her.

"Want an Advil?" she asked, when the conversation grew stale.

"What?"

"For your headache. Just remembered I had them."

"Oh. Not while I'm drinking. Thanks." They had, by this time, downed a third of the bottle without really noticing. Kit was larger than Val, but she had a better tolerance, and they were both at a pleasant juncture in the course of inebriation.

"I've still got Doug's coke, you know."

"Who?"

"That guy from the train. Seeing him again reminded me. We could do it, you know. Why not? We could stay up and map out a book on the cave. We should write one together."

He'd never taken cocaine before, though he'd had a few friends who favored it in undergrad. Now he was a father and it seemed a little late to start, but the unreality of the circumstances seemed to make him unreal too, and he behaved as he would in a dream.

Though drunk, they hesitated a moment in the bathroom before preparing the cocaine. The absurdity of the situation embarrassed them. Without acknowledging it, Val tapped the powder out on the counter, cut it ineptly into lines with her university ID while Kit watched.

"I thought you'd be better at this," he said, mainly for an excuse to say anything at all.

"Why? What do you think my life is?"

Kit shrugged, handed her a hundred-ruble note he'd rolled into a tube on her instruction.

The powder burned when he snorted it. The rush came very quickly after the burn, and he was surprised at how altered he felt after just a few minutes. But then the nasal passage, he reasoned, was very close to the brain. Val had been going on about cultural rituals, ritual objects, how they related to snorting coke in bathrooms. Kit told her to write it down, and she agreed but made no move to do so.

"It's the handling," he said. "I mean, the *handing*. The handing back and forth. It's something about the handing things around that bonds people."

"We are our hands."

"Yes. The handprints on the wall. Through millennia."

"Write *that* down."

They were speaking very quickly, sitting on the tiled floor of the half bathroom. Neither had a pen, or paper, or any desire to retrieve these items.

"Do you think we'll be famous?" Kit found himself asking.

"No. Maybe George will."

"You've gone off him."

"I think. I don't know. Ambition is a corruption of love, you know?"

"What?"

"I don't even know. I think there's something going on. I think maybe he's . . . I don't even know. It seems crazy."

Suddenly Kit stood, restless and claustrophobic, and Val followed suit.

They found Mark in the living room, hands folded, deep in thought. He looked too big for the room, like Alice after drinking her potion. Kit wasn't sure he was glad to see him.

"Oh," said Mark, looking up at them, "there you are."

"Were you looking for us?" asked Kit.

"No."

Val turned to leave, but paused when Mark spoke again. "Sorry if I've been a bit strange lately."

Val laughed, and Mark looked affronted. "No, no." She crossed her wrists in front of her, an odd gesture. "I'm laughing at myself. We're all strange. I've been strange. I mean, you don't need to apologize. Or maybe we all do, all the time."

Mark smiled. "Very Catholic of you."

"I'm not—oh."

Kit moved to settle on the couch by Mark, willing himself to act naturally and incurring the opposite effect. He was too stiff and jittery at the same time, as if his body were vibrating. Val seemed to fare a little better, but she was used to this sort of thing.

"What's going on?" Mark asked.

Kit shrugged.

"Nothing," said Val, with too much emphasis.

Mark watched them for a moment. "Are you on drugs?"

"What?" asked Kit. Val had started to laugh again.

"It's kind of obvious."

"Guess it was good stuff," said Val.

"You didn't take drugs through customs, did you? Do you know how dangerous that is? Here, of all places? Not just to you, but to this entire enterprise?" This was aimed squarely at Val. Mark had clocked her immediately as the source of the contraband.

"Relax," said Kit. "It was the guy on the train."

Mark sat back, disapproving and slightly hurt. "You took something he gave you?"

"You want some?"

Mark shook his head. "Of course not."

His reaction was strong enough to make Kit doubt his judgment for a moment, though this was quickly replaced by a pang of annoyance. Why did Mark always have to make such a show of it? Such a theatrical performance of good sense.

"You know what's really weird?" said Val, who was either oblivious to the moment of tension or pretending to be. "I saw him the other day in Yakutsk."

Mark turned sharply toward her. "You saw him too?"

"Yeah, he grabbed my shopping list and said it was spy code. And he mentioned his business partner *Vasiliy*. Isn't that weird?"

"It's not that weird," said Kit.

"Doug," said Mark.

"Yeah." Val stood to pace.

"Vasiliy is one of maybe five names guys can have in Russia, so it's really not weird," Kit insisted.

Val shrugged. "I guess. But I mean, Vasiliy's sketchy, right? And Doug was talking about how they're gonna buy the forests and cut them down for wood and turn them into farmland after global warming. Which seems completely like something Vasiliy would do. And George, I don't even know. I don't even know what's going on."

"Clearly you've thought about it," said Kit. His annoyance was no longer contained to Mark; it eclipsed their earlier camaraderie. He wanted to be free of these people, free of responsibility for problems that had no connection to his real life. But then, what had he heard earlier that evening? Hadn't he been thinking something similar?

"I didn't see Doug," said Mark. "I saw the other guy."

"What?" asked Val.

"Klaus Kinski."

"Oh," said Val, with interest. "How weird."

"It was."

"Did you say hi?"

Kit watched as Mark and Val shared a laugh. Not a common occurrence.

"Imagine taking coke from Klaus Kinski."

"Imagine taking coke from Doug."

This would usually have set her on edge, but in her altered state, she took on a confiding tone, which seemed to pacify Mark further. "No, you might think it would be a bad idea, but he's the perfect kind of person for it. Always a gamble, of course, but it's good stuff."

"I can see that."

"You sure you don't want a bump?"

"I'm sure."

Kit felt unfairly cut out of this conversation by his first-class train ticket. He'd had a strange encounter too, after all, not two hours ago. Though his was more alarming than salacious. "I heard Vasiliy and George talking," he said. "I went to Vasiliy's office, and I heard them talking about . . ." He paused. It was hard to say it out loud. Mark and Val waited. "Something living in the forest," he said finally, feeling less ridiculous than he'd expected to. "He said, 'They're from the hills. They'll go back up. You'll never see them coming.'"

Neither replied for a moment. Val had stopped pacing but was wringing her hands in a very distracting manner. Mark, usually the fidgeter, was still.

"Well," said Val, "I'm glad you finally said it. That something weird is happening."

"But who's coming?"

"Wolves. Bears. Nomads . . ." Mark trailed off.

"You know, George has cameras up in the woods. I've seen him go off to check them."

"*That*'s where he goes?"

"He told me he was scouting out locations."

"What else did they say?" Mark asked. "Vasiliy and George, I mean."

Kit told them, not bothering to cover up the fact that he had listened at the door.

"It's land," said Val, when he'd finished. "They want farmland, or lumber. Or something else. For money. People always fight about money."

"They?" asked Kit.

"Interested parties, I guess."

"George has money," said Mark.

Val shrugged. She had made a few half laps from one side of the couch to the other and now sat on its arm.

"*Having money* is not always the same as having money," explained Kit.

"Well," said Val, "nothing is how it's supposed to be. We can admit that now, can't we?"

The two men looked at her, and she stood up again, as if to make a speech.

"We can," said Kit, when no speech came.

"Well." She sat back down.

For a moment, they were silent, thinking.

Mark was the first to speak. "It's a conspiracy then."

They all laughed, because they were rational people whose professional lives were not supposed to include plots and intrigue, and because they were afraid. And then, again, they lapsed into silence, considering. Kit felt jumpy, the conversation full of stops and starts. He wished he hadn't snorted the coke and that he wasn't having this conversation now, though he suspected that the former was necessary for the latter. The things he was saying had felt impossible to say before, even to himself.

"You can reach a point," he said, "when not believing is more credulous than believing."

Val nodded. "When you look at the evidence."

"The place feels wrong," Kit added.

Mark laughed with more discomfort than before. "You're on drugs. You should hear yourselves."

"Yes," said Val, "but think about it."

He did think, in a slow, careful way. Kit watched him work through it. Finally he shook his head without much conviction. "So you think, to be clear, that we've been brought here under false pretenses. That there's some plot. Or something else. You're saying two different things. About the land and money and about *people in the woods.*" He rushed the last part of the statement, as if to minimize its impact.

He made a good point. It was advantageous, Kit saw, to have a sober person around for these revelations. After thinking for a moment, Kit turned to Val. "Has George told you anything?"

"What do you mean?"

"When you talked to him alone."

This was the first allusion to the affair to pass between the three of them, the first direct acknowledgment that Val was in a position to know more about George's machinations. But as it turned out, she did not. She paused, slightly affronted, before shaking her head. "He just talks about the future and the past and everything on a very grand scale. It feels like he's repeating lecture openers he's got stored up."

Kit laughed, enjoying the meanness of this, then looked around the room as if George might walk in. His presence in the house occurred to all of them at once, and they became cautious.

"When I saw him check the cameras," Val continued, in a lower tone, "he freaked out on me. Screaming. His face was different. It was scary."

"Maybe we should just stay here. Stay back and go home," Kit said.

Mark looked as if the option had never occurred to him. "I guess."

"Because it's all too bizarre. There's too much wrong." As he spoke, his mind drifted back to the painted cave. The reds and ochers and blacks undulating on its walls. It was more beautiful than anything he'd ever seen. And it would belong to him, in some way, when they presented their discovery. The others, he felt, had to be thinking of it too.

"We could go back," said Val, slowly, "but with a plan."

"Well, there's the radio. I can use it, I think," Kit suggested.

"Good, okay."

"We can't exactly leave a discovery of this magnitude in the hands of somebody whose motivations we don't know," Mark reasoned.

Kit nodded. "And if anything goes wrong, we can radio for help."

They didn't go into what, exactly, could go wrong. The moment for honesty about their fears had passed. They were rational people who made plans. But of course, Kit's mind couldn't help but recur to what remained unspoken. Not in theories but images: patterns in the dirt, shadows crossing in front of his tent, George's face changing in a way Val had only half explained. He thought of the dense tree line, crevices in the mountain face. *You'll never see them coming.* Was that what George had said? It already felt unreal.

The next day, Vasiliy drove them to the airfield in near silence and gave George a cold goodbye. He ignored Mark and Val, though he'd done this consistently since they met, and neither attempted to interact with him. Kit was granted an ambiguous smile.

George did not attempt to hide his irritation with Vasiliy but did not explain it either. He sat quietly on the plane, looking over maps.

15

ANATOLIY WANTED TO TALK AS HE FLEW THEM BACK OUT TO the Malova Valley, which suited Val fine. He had a gift for filling silences, and she was happy to drop an occasional log on the fire in the form of a question. She could focus on his stories surprisingly well in spite of a pounding headache.

There had been a moment, just before she'd boarded the plane, when she'd contemplated refusing to get on—faking illness or even just telling the truth. She'd looked back at Kit, who appeared genuinely queasy at the sight of the plane, and Mark, who was busy picking at his fingernails, then walked on. George had motioned for her to sit by him, and she did so. Now he sat with his knee touching hers, looking over a map as Anatoliy told them about the movie he'd seen that weekend, a romantic comedy called *Phoenix, Philadelphia* in which a woman has to choose between a junior congressman and the lead singer in a rock band. "And who do you think she choose?" he asked Val.

"Who does she like more?"

"She likes them both. This is her trouble."

"Well, the congressman—is he a liberal or a conservative?"

Anatoliy thought for a moment. "This does not matter for her. He is wanting to make things better for everyday people. And he has airplane too."

"Is he the one from Phoenix? Or Philadelphia?"

"Phoenix."

Val had absorbed the same miasmic knowledge of smaller American cities through media as most Anglo-Canadians, but she'd heard about Phoenix in particular from Lily, who spent a sweltering summer there with a boyfriend who bought and sold scrap metal. "She picks the singer."

"Yes! He is childhood sweetheart, but then his group 'blow up overnight.' She think he does not love her now. He can have any girl. But then he says that famous hit single is for her."

"And the congressman?"

Anatoliy shrugged. "He has job. He is okay."

"I hate those stupid movies," said Mark.

They watched as Anatoliy's plane gathered speed along the unforested strip by the face of the mountain. It did not look like an ideal runway, but Anatoliy lifted off without issue. The sky was filled with dark clouds that morning, and soon the An-2 disappeared into them. After Anatoliy had gone, leaving them with crates of fresh supplies in the clearing next to their campsite, an air of caution crept over them. The noises of the forest that had become familiar now sounded eerie again, louder than she'd remembered, and the dark tree line seemed to have edged in closer during their absence. The camp, half dismantled, felt uncanny after a weekend away, not quite theirs anymore. Nobody spoke as they repitched their tents.

Kit in particular looked spooked. His face was damp, slightly haggard. She thought he'd only been worried by the bush plane, but this proved to be only part of the problem. His hangovers apparently took a psychological form as well as a physical one. He kept looking at patterns in the dirt and hovered for a while over the satellite radio, which they'd left behind for the weekend after some discussion over its weight. Val made a note to ask him how it worked, exactly, as only he and George knew how to operate it.

Though uneasy all morning, she was only really frightened when she realized *why* she wanted to learn how to work the radio. In the back of her mind, a scenario had been playing out unacknowledged in which something terrible happened, and she was forced to radio for help alone. The insanity of it hit her at once. *And she had gone back.* Of course, they had very little solid information. Only a few unlikely occurrences, loose ends, phrases overheard through doors. All she knew was that something was not as it was supposed to be, and now she was stuck here.

If Mark was having similar thoughts, he commanded them better. Though he'd agreed to work and communicate with Kit and Val in Yakutsk, he was now summarily ignoring them unless addressed directly. Kit was in his tent. She tried not to look at George, who was unpacking supplies next to Mark.

They had a short, pleasureless lunch of beans with toast, peanuts, and electrolyte powder dissolved into water. Mark ate in his tent, and Val wished she could do the same. The men's expressions made her uneasy. She could feel something passing between the two of them as she pushed the beans around on her tin plate.

She wasn't eager to return to the cave. Considering the importance of their find, the rarity and the great beauty of it, her reluctance surprised her. But she found herself afraid to see it again, afraid it wouldn't be as astonishing on a second look, or that it would. Or, though this was ridiculous, that it might simply be gone when she looked again. Mark and Kit seemed to share her hesitance. Kit made no motion to go, and Mark didn't stir from his tent until specifically called.

Only George was immune. He rounded them up and set them to work lighting the passage to the cave. They lugged a generator up and hooked it to a series of small lights staked into the ground on either side of the path. Those they couldn't beat into the ground, owing to the presence of calcite buildup or stone, had to be installed in little mounds of earth brought in from the excavation pits, as George had forgotten to buy any sort of stands to prop them up.

It was dull, grueling work and took longer than expected. Kit lagged behind, moody and hungover, which Val felt gave her permission to do the same occasionally. Mark, proper farm boy that he was, did twice his share of the labor. George worked diligently alongside them, though Val wondered if this was just as much to make sure they didn't talk to one another as to finish the work on time. They slept that night as if rehearsing for death.

The next day, they began to clear the avalanche. George drilled a hole into the cracked calcite surrounding one of the rocks at the top of the pile and screwed a hook into it. The others stood at a wary distance. He then attached the winch—a simple, leverage-based tool powered by gas—to the hook. The cable was long, and he unraveled it for about twenty feet, as far as he could go before the passage started to curve, then turned on the machine. The winch looked as if it had been made during Khrushchev's tenure and had been in regular use since. It was dinged in a few places, with chipped paint, and smelled of stale gasoline. George had explained that it should topple the rocks one by one, without causing any greater structural collapse.

This precarious arrangement would almost certainly not have met CCOHS requirements, was very likely illegal by whatever standards the Russians had in place, and genuinely unnerved everyone involved. George joked that the university would fire him if it heard about it, and this was possibly true.

George operated the device himself. He told the others to stand back at a greater distance, and they obliged. Val could only partly see, at her angle in the passage, as the first rock came unstuck. The thud of it toppling echoed through the cave. Val turned away. There was something macabre about the scene. The next rock, heavier and more awkwardly shaped, was trickier. The winch strained. George drilled more holes, readjusted, and tried again. Still, the cable vibrated with tension.

The cable snapped quickly, almost silently, at the base of the winch. Val, who had been thinking more about the philosophical implications of the process than the practicalities, didn't fully understand what had happened for a second, until George swore, loudly. "The bastards scammed me," he said, more than once, picking up the limp cable, then dropping it and examining the unmoved rock, the snapped cord still dangling from it. After a moment he stalked off, saying he needed to take a walk to figure out what to do next. The others, none of whom had spoken or moved much during the two minutes it took for this scene to unfold, watched him leave. Mark examined the winch just as George had done and confirmed to the other two that it was indeed broken, though neither had doubted it.

They walked back awkwardly to the camp together. "Maybe he'll just pack up for now," said Val. Kit shrugged, and Mark seemed to exert some willpower in refusing to argue. There was nothing to do at camp. Kit went to take a nap, and Mark, to read his book by the unlit fire. Val tried to read in her tent, felt dirty, and decided to wash in the river.

She walked down to the place where the water was slow and shallow, and left her clothes on a rock. The white, shining sky reflected on the rippling water, making the light of the surface very bright, the shadows a deep black. A river comprising day and night, knocking together, pushing apart, repulsing each other like mismatched magnets. She stepped in very quickly and dove under. The cold stung, but it was better not to hesitate.

Underwater, she closed her eyes, listening to the pulse of the river. The river was very shallow where she stood, and she had to crouch to fully immerse herself. Her toes dug into the cool clay of the riverbed, searching for stones. The hard part done, she grabbed her soap tin from the rock she'd left it on, at the water's edge, and began to wash herself.

As she ran soap over her arms, she heard a movement in the trees and saw, in a bush on the opposite bank of the river, a pair of large, wet black eyes staring out. The eyes were not attached to a face but staring disembodied from the bush. She remained perfectly still. The eyes held hers for a moment, and then they were gone. It took her another moment to react. She got out without finishing her bath and, although the eyes did not reappear, threw her clothes on without bothering to dry off.

There was something in the Bible about this. Something about a bush with eyes. God appearing to Moses as a burning bush. Moses asking, *What are you?* The bush responding, *I am that I am*. Well, she'd always pictured it with eyes, at least. But this was all nonsense—a consequence of her conversation with Kit and Mark, and of the relentless light. She hadn't been sleeping well.

In the safety of her tent, toweling off her hair, she thought, *Visual hallucinations are not uncommon, especially in periods of heightened stress.*

And then: *If it's all over, at least I've done something with my life.*

⚘

George was still gone when she returned, Kit still asleep, Mark still reading *STALIN*. She sat by him and offered him some almonds she'd bought in Yakutsk, which he accepted. "I'll bet he's looking at those cameras," he said. She nodded. The thought had occurred to her too.

"We should be doing something," she said, knowing she sounded stupid. "He shouldn't treat the site that way. And where *is* he?"

Mark pointed up at the sky, where a few dark clouds had moved in. "It's going to rain. Let's make sure we're not leaving anything out to get soaked."

Though of course this didn't address the *something* Val had been talking about, it was concrete action, and they did it efficiently, moving the portable stove and a few loose supplies into the storage shed. Soon after they'd finished, the rain did begin to fall.

"Do you think he's okay?" Val asked.

Mark shrugged. "He's gone through worse than rain, I think."

He turned to retreat to his tent.

"If he doesn't come back," she called after him, "we radio for a plane."

She found Kit lying down in his tent and staring at the raindrops hitting its red nylon wall. He said he had a headache, with nausea, and she offered him a cigarette. He took one drag then handed it back. It only made the sensation stronger. His hand, as it brushed hers, was hot. Before leaving, she gave him an Advil, which he swallowed dry.

Rain had fallen occasionally in short, torrential bursts throughout the weeks, and at first it seemed to follow the same pattern, but this time the downpour didn't stop. A deluge. Val kept expecting it to stop as suddenly as it had started, but it kept coming. George was still out there. She wondered if he'd found somewhere to take shelter, if rain even bothered him. She worried about the paintings too. They hadn't been careful enough, pulling down the avalanche. There had been a hole near the top of it before, but what if George had destabilized it? It was wild that they were working so close to an internal avalanche in the first place, however old, and even wilder that they'd simply accepted that condition until now. Kit understood the geological aspects of the work better than she did, and she'd ask him if the pictographs were at risk when he felt better.

After some two hours in which Mark did not come to find her in order to figure out the radio, as she thought they'd agreed on, she ducked through the rain to check in on Kit again. He was asleep and didn't wake when she said his name.

She resolved to find Mark next and saw him stalking back into the camp, entirely drenched, as soon as she unzipped the tent. "Where were you?" she called.

He shrugged, then motioned for her to join him at the radio.

"Where's Kit?" he asked, when she reached him at the center of the camp, under the radio's canopy. She stood to the side, trying not to drip on the equipment.

"Where were *you*?" she asked again.

"I went to look for him."

This was stupid, but she felt too tired to remind him of it. He must have known he was behaving irrationally and decided to continue. She didn't want any reminders about the Eagle Scouts that a conversation of this nature would incur.

"Didn't find him," he added. "Do you know how to work this thing?"

"No."

"Kit does."

"He's asleep. Like sick asleep. With a fever, I think."

"He seemed fine before," Mark insisted.

"He said he wasn't feeling well in Yakutsk."

"What's the incubation period for malaria?"

But this was ridiculous. "Malaria? We're in Siberia."

"We're taking quinine."

"For insurance purposes. That's what George said."

"Oh, well, that settles it then."

"It's not malaria."

"It was endemic among rail workers on the Trans-Siberian. It's entirely possible."

"You read that in *STALIN*?" There was an edge to her voice now, and he was quick to match her tone.

"Yes, and it happens to be relevant. There's a purpose to educating yourself broadly."

After this, the fight left them. George was gone. Kit had been struck ill in a possibly malarial and distinctly biblical way. As if he'd been smote. Neither Mark nor Val knew how to operate the satellite radio. They listened for a moment to the sound of the rain.

"I saw something watching me," Val said nervously. "Down by the river."

"A deer, or some other prey animal. That's what it almost always is when you feel something watching you in the woods."

Having overstepped already in a moment when panic was not an option, she did not clarify that she had not felt eyes on her but rather seen them. They decided to try to rouse Kit and see if they could cajole him into operating the radio.

He was still asleep when they returned to him, did not stir when Mark called his name, and simply rolled over when he shook him. Eventually Mark half dragged him through the mud, with Val trailing behind. The rain having woken him up some, he turned a few knobs when they explained what they needed him to do, only to be met with static. "They're gone, or they're ignoring us."

Val walked him back to his tent, then tried to figure out the instruction manual with Mark. The results were the same, and they argued only perfunctorily. "He'll be better tomorrow. He knows how to do it when he's focused," Val said eventually. Mark nodded.

It was a mutual acknowledgment that they had no idea what to do next and could only try to sleep. Val lay awake, irritated by a migrating itch. Each time she tried to scratch it, it reappeared in another spot on her body.

16

THE WOMB, WARM AROUND HIM: HE CURLED INTO IT. HE WAS dying and now saw that death was not a push forward but a drift backward, to a pre-birth state. This was a breakthrough. He had to tell Min-Seo. Tell everyone. He could write a paper. But first, to escape the death womb. His muscles were weak, and he couldn't orient himself in space. He fell asleep, or rather fell into sleep, like a stone dropped in a lake.

When he woke up, Val was sitting near him. "Where are we?" he asked.

"You're sick," she said. "You have a fever." The unrelenting light throbbed through the red nylon of the tent, casting a pink glow over Val's face. He really had been out of it. Could a fever give him brain damage? Christ. Where was his wife?

"She's at work."

"What?"

"You asked for Melissa."

"For who?"

"You said you wanted your wife."

He laughed. "Melissa. Me*lis*sa. Oh God." Min-Seo would be home soon. She was angry with him. "I don't have to explain this to you," she'd said. And she didn't. He knew she was angry because he'd left the baby alone, with nobody to watch him. He could die out there. He'd drown. "Oh God. Jesus. I'm sorry."

"It's all right," said Val. "Nobody's angry with you."

"My baby is alone. He could *die*," he cried.

"No, no. Nobody's dying. He's at home. He's watching TV, okay? With his mom."

"Oh." That was solved, at least. But how would he get out of here? He could barely move, and there was something very important he had to do. Something to tell someone. Oh God. They'd made a terrible mistake, coming back here. He'd known it was wrong. "They'll be coming for us soon. For the needle too."

"It's fine, it's fine. Nobody's coming for you."

"Now they'll kill us and nobody will find the bodies. We'll be like—oh God, who was it?"

"Amelia Earhart?"

"Rockefeller. Like Michael Rockefeller. They'll hide our bones!"

She gave him a pill, which he tried, with abrupt docility, to swallow. It lodged in his throat, and the water she poured down after it nearly drowned him. He coughed and curled into himself, clutching weakly at his aching ribs. "Oh *God*."

Unable to stay still in her own tent any longer, Val went back to Kit's, partly to keep an eye on him and partly to stave off the terror she felt when alone. When he woke up delirious at sunrise, talking about death and curses, she willed herself not to think about George or the radio. She tried to soothe him. It was something to do, anyway.

She had some experience with fever ravings, having spent time with habitual drug users. She knew not to try to reason with a disjointed mind. Just stay and say the simplest, most reassuring thing. But when Kit said, "They'll be coming for us," she thought back to the wet black eyes she'd seen in the bush. *Maybe they* are *after us—whatever* they *are.*

Still, it seemed more productive to focus on the immediate issue. Kit was in bad shape. He was soaked in sweat with a high fever and a tenuous hold on reality. The first aid kit was in the supply shed. At the very least she'd find a thermometer and more Advil there.

The sun was still rising, the rain still falling. She felt, as she moved to unzip the tent, that to do so would be very wrong. Dangerous. She lay back down and told Kit, who was still talking softly to himself, to be quiet. Were there footsteps? Was George back? Someone, she sensed, was there. But she could hear nothing through the rain, see no shadows through the nylon in the weak light. After a while, she lay back. Though still unwilling to open the tent, her certainty was gone.

She slept only a couple of hours, then stayed with Kit for a couple more. Lily had always found comfort in having Val near her when she was sick. The rain kept coming, and Val tried to listen through it for George's footsteps, but the sound never came. Kit slept for a while, then clawed his way back into consciousness, jabbering again about Michael Rockefeller and the people who wanted to get them.

"They'll be coming. We won't even hear them. They're too agile. They'll come at night."

"Who?" she asked finally. "Who's coming?"

He said nothing for a moment, then, fearfully, "Those creatures. The curse. It's all true. Can't you see it?"

Val shivered. It did make some sense, if you placed yourself into the mind of a delirious fever patient. They had been told the place was cursed. Or *occupied*, which was somehow worse. From the beginning, she'd been pushing down some feeling of guilt, an atmosphere of trespass. And under this, a primal fear.

She read aloud to him for a while from *Wuthering Heights*. She'd been carrying it around, intending to read it for weeks.

"'I discerned, obscurely, a child's face looking through the window. Terror made me cruel; and, finding it useless to attempt shaking the creature off, I pulled its wrist on to the broken pane, and rubbed it to and fro till the blood ran down and soaked the bedclothes: still it wailed, "Let me in!" and maintained its tenacious gripe, almost maddening me with fear'—God, I forgot how disturbing this was. I read it in high school."

Kit rolled away, and she shut the book.

The rain had fallen through the long twilight and the brief night. The creatures had come, as Kit had known they would. He couldn't say when they came or how long they stayed. Time had collapsed. At one point, he'd seen a hand touch his tent. There was a little light then. They must have come with some light still in the sky or stayed until it returned. The hand was not violent. It moved its fingers slowly along the fabric. The rain ran between the ridges of its fingerprints—he could see these prints very clearly and part of a face behind them too. The rest in shadow. He could have reached up and joined his hand to the other, with only the red veil between them. He didn't, though. He lay perfectly still, pulling all his muscles inward toward his heart.

It moved on eventually. He could see them pacing. Saw their shadows moving, even through the dark. His eyes were stronger, somehow, than they'd ever been in his life. And his ears too. He heard their toes in the mud, the swinging of the shed door, the distant whispers in a low, droning language. He prayed he would live. He didn't hear them leave. For a long time he lay on his back, listening to the rain, and then this stopped too. Only a strange white noise remained, like a wave forever crashing. Perhaps he was dead already. And then a voice, alarmed, calling out: "What?!"

At first, Mark thought there must have been a hurricane. The camp was wrecked. The shed door flung open, boxes of tools emptied outside it. But this was not a random disaster. For one thing, their tents were left untouched. The radio too seemed intact, though it was emitting a constant static. And there were footprints in the mud, their outlines blurred by the rain, but their shapes distinct enough: bare feet. So many trails of footprints, tracing back and forth through the camp, beating tunnels into the mud. People had been here, a number of them.

He stepped cautiously from his tent and turned in a tight circle. The rain had ceased. The day was bright and fresh, very still. Was he alone now? Where were the others? Had they taken them? Who had his brain just unquestioningly referenced as *they*? Just as these thoughts occurred to him, Val poked her head sleepily out of Kit's tent. "What do you mean, 'what'?"

He must have spoken. He turned to her, stunned, and said nothing, letting her see for herself. Shock and horror played across her face. She looked for a long time, then pointed to one set of tracks in the mud.

They were more distinct than the others, geometric. The prints of rubber-soled work boots. "George," she said. "He's been here."

With their eyes, they followed the tracks, flanked by a pair of less distinct prints, to George's tent, positioned a little bit away from camp. It had been stripped, the pelts removed to leave only a wooden skeleton. Papers in the mud. The electric typewriter drowned and half submerged in the unsteady ground.

Past this ruin, the prints led away from the camp in the same direction as the murky, dull footprints that covered the campground floor. With an unexpected, distant self-possession, he bent to examine them. Though their quality had been degraded, he could make out the impressions of toes on some of the intruders' prints. While some seemed to wear shoes, others must have been barefoot. As he realized this, he had to quell all dread and confusion that the fact inspired. He needed to focus. Had they forced George to go with them? Were they George's feet at all? These were made by his boots, almost certainly, but they could have been taken from his feet.

There was no use in speculation or commentary. They had to figure out what to do. They had to act. "The radio is broken," said Mark. It seemed the most relevant thing to say.

"I heard them," said Kit. "They smashed it in with a rock."

"The flare gun," Val suggested, with the startled tone of sudden recollection.

Mark nodded. "If they haven't taken it."

The flare gun was their backup safety plan, as rehearsed in Canada. They'd been told repeatedly where it was kept and how to use it, all while being reassured that of course they'd never need to. In an absolute worst-case scenario that certainly would not occur, they were to shoot the flare gun straight up into the air and wait for help. If nobody else saw it, Anatoliy's old air force friend had a farm about seventy-five miles away, and he, along with his family and farmhands, had been instructed to keep a lookout for any signal of distress from the direction of the camp. These people would then, hopefully, radio for Anatoliy.

Unfortunately, like every other piece of equipment on the dig, it was kept in the storage shed and might have been stolen, or else lodged in the mud. He was startled to realize how makeshift the entire operation was. George's confidence had left no room for questions.

Mark, having been subject to a rural Alaskan childhood, had seen flare guns before. Most of them were bright orange, almost like water guns. For whatever reason, the flare gun George or the University of Toronto had provided was black, compact, and sinister. "Well, it couldn't hurt to check," Mark said.

He and Val trudged together through the mud to the shed, both carrying bear spray. Neither mentioned it, of course, but the possibility remained unspoken between them: *What if somebody's still in there?* Mark had thought, for some reason, that the door had been ripped off its hinges, but when he looked at it now, he saw it was merely swung open, ominous, indifferent. Inside it was dark. Neither moved for a moment.

Eventually, Val stepped an inch into the doorway and shined her flashlight on the area. He felt a wave of relief when nothing moved, then a wave of shame at his own inaction. "Don't touch anything yet."

The shed had been entirely overturned: boxes moved around and emptied, shelves cleared. He wondered at first how he hadn't heard this happen, but on second observation, he perceived a deliberate quality to the scene. What was not missing from the shed was eerily rearranged. Boxes of stone artifacts, brushes, and north arrows had been rearranged by a strange logic of shape and texture. All spare trowels had been taken, and tent stakes too. Gingerly, they began to sift through upturned boxes and scattered items for the flare gun. Mark noticed, with a pang of horror, that their water was gone entirely, but didn't mention it to Val, who was stacking empty boxes in a corner to clear their view. She found the gun, eventually, in an otherwise empty box.

"Good," said Mark, bewildered. "Good."

She handed it to him quickly, happy to relinquish responsibility. "You've shot a gun, right? In America?"

"A hunting rifle. But I'll do it. Don't worry."

"Okay."

"Do you have earplugs? I need some."

She brought two pairs from her tent and stayed out for some reason to watch him shoot the flare. He wished she wouldn't. He didn't feel comfortable holding the flare gun—this was only natural with a piece of equipment he'd never used before, but it was still awful even then for her to see him look awkward holding the gun. Still, he told her to stand at a distance, then steadied his arm and shot with something resembling confidence. The screech of the flare gun rattled his skull, and even with the earplugs in, he found himself bringing his left hand to his ear. He turned to look up at the stalk of fire shooting up into the clear sky. It burned outward from its core, leaving behind smoke and ash, which began to fall softly toward the ground.

It had not shot very high. He thought it very unlikely that anybody would see it. Anybody whom they wanted alerted to their presence, at least. He was debating whether to tell Val this or to let her keep her hope, when she sighed and called the whole thing pointless.

They began, with equal parts fear and awkwardness, to walk back to camp. Mark wondered briefly if Kit would still be there when they returned, then pronounced the thought ridiculous.

"It was strange," said Val, "that those items were all mixed up like that in the storage shed. Why would a person do that." This last sentence should have been a question, but her voice was flat with a strained effort toward neutrality.

"To fuck with people, I guess. KGB."

"Or CIA."

He shrugged.

"The toes, though. The footprints had *toes.*"

"They make shoes with bare footprints printed on the soles, you know. To throw you off." Mark had seen this in a movie once.

Val didn't reply.

"I'm more concerned with the water." Mark knew he'd said this only to feel less silly, as if she could tell his earlier information came from a spy movie. She had a strange ability, he'd always felt, of reading his mind with the least generous interpretation possible. Still, he regretted the admission when he saw her face.

She stopped walking. "What?"

"They took the water."

"They took the *water*?"

He felt it best not to respond, until, unable to help himself, he added, "Dehydration is a greater and more immediate risk than parasites. We can go to the river for more water."

Val fished a beaten pack of cigarettes from her pocket and began to smoke one. The cigarette itself seemed suited to the situation—slightly misshapen and bent downward, like a drooping weed. Mark too seemed to droop with despair, whenever he let his thoughts drift. He spent considerable energy forcing his spine to straighten and his thoughts to arrange themselves logically. As they reached the camp, he had come to a decision about how to act and said so. "You have your bear spray and I have mine," he told Val. "I should walk toward the farm for help. You wait here with Kit. If anyone comes, you tell them about me, and if I reach people first, I'll tell them about you. That's what makes most sense."

Before he left, he went with Val to get water. She said she felt watched by the river. After that, he took a quarter of an hour to gather what supplies he could and set off. Val wished him luck, and he decided, given the circumstances, that she was not saying this sarcastically. He said goodbye to Kit in his tent and got no reply. He just kept sleeping and sweating profusely. The forest still seemed too quiet. It would be best, he felt, not to dawdle.

17

Val had wanted to be alone, but once Mark left she realized the oppressive presence of another consciousness had been the only thing keeping her mind clear. She couldn't really freak out in front of him. Now, with just a delirious Kit, she was afraid to even speak for fear of succumbing fully to panic. She sat in Kit's tent, listening to the breeze in a state of high alarm for some time. Eventually she exhausted her focus, and her mind began to wander.

She was worried about George, whether he was alive or dead. She had tried to keep her mind off this before, as pointless as it was. She understood now that she hadn't known him at all. That there was something frightening and incomprehensible in him. And still she admired him. Still wanted to hold him, to hear him speak. She wished he was there, even with his opaque motives. At least he brought certainty. That seemed to matter more than good intentions. She probably would have let him drown her in the river, so long as he was telling her everything was fine and there was a perfectly logical reason for the drowning.

But no.

This was exactly the sort of thinking she needed to guard against. She wanted to live. In any case, she did not want to be killed. And it would be terrible for Kit, who had a baby and a real life. Positive thoughts eluding her, she counted her own breaths for some time until she heard, at a distance, what sounded like a baby crying.

It was a piercing, painful wail. Evolutionarily, she'd read, women were supposed to hate the cry of an infant more than any other noise. It was designed to be terrible enough to demand attention and also to elicit immediate maternal concern. It accomplished this, though infused with intense confusion and alarm.

She was not hallucinating. Kit heard it too. "I'll get him," he said, before rolling over.

Val tried to rationalize the noise as the call of a fox or some other forest creature, unknown but necessarily harmless. But as it grew steadily louder, it became even more undeniably human in origin. Val remembered ghost stories about monsters in the woods mimicking the wails of little children, luring unsuspecting hunters to their deaths.

"Can you get him this time?" asked Kit.

The cry, though it never ceased, stopped growing louder. Val remained still. Footsteps, closer and closer to her, could be heard heading away from it. Decisive, confident, striding. She knew them.

"It's George," she said to Kit. The sound of her own voice surprised her by its flatness. "He's alive."

This elicited no response.

"He's alive," she said again, this time to herself, and unzipped the tent.

There he was, advancing toward her. She had known him after all. The strange cry kept up in the background, steady except for occasional gasping pauses. George did not seem to notice it. He moved steadily toward her. His bearing, always erect, now seemed almost unearthly, as if a string tied to his heart were pulling him up toward the sun. Productless, his black hair fell across his forehead like tousled bangs—almost a child's haircut. His linen shirt hung limp, smeared with mud, torn at the shoulder, and hanging open. Its abalone buttons had all been torn off. A pale patch on his wrist where his watch had been. A layer of sweat, fresh on his face, making him glow. His eyes seemed wetter, darker, more prominent than before. They shined with inner purpose. And he was smiling.

He settled his face into something more professional when he met her. "Val," he said, "there have been some unexpected but exciting developments."

Mark felt he was making good time, though he couldn't be sure. He had a watch now and a compass, but no pedometer. The land was unfamiliar to him. He'd taken the topographical maps, but they were not meant to be used for ground directions and there were no features along his route distinct enough to reference as landmarks yet. Though starting from the edge of the valley, he did not want to cross over the mountains immediately, keeping instead to the trees until he was closer to his destination. There was, once he'd walked a few miles from camp, no clear delineation between trees and mountain either. They seemed to climb up the small mountains indefinitely at some points.

Sometimes the trees were too close together, the forest floor too thick with needles, causing him to sink six inches every time he stepped down. The ground was uneven too, snow having pushed the soil into small hills and valleys in the winter. His calves ached; his arms were scraped from squeezing between trees when walking around a fresh summer thicket would have taken too long. This reminded him of reconnaissance and how much he'd despised it. He was aware too that every clumsy step might alert *them*. The unknown enemy. The ones he could not or would not name.

Some internal drive propelled him forward. It was easier now that he was moving. Though he registered every distant sound, fear had given way to a state of blank alertness. He spent hours like this, focusing only on his compass and the conservation of water. He would cross a stream soon, if his map was accurate. If he had been thinking about anything more than that, he would have thought that the world could in fact be very simple and concrete.

For much of human history, this state of clarity would have been familiar. Ego shelved, instinct leading. Now he understood Valerie's yearning for a time before invention, which he'd once termed sentimental. If this had been what she'd meant, he could see the allure.

"What happened to you?" Val asked, gesturing vaguely at George's little-boy hair, his ruined shirt. His signet ring was gone too, she realized.

"I've made contact. They were very drawn to the shell buttons. It's funny—the buttons never occurred to me as a possible offering, but immediately they wanted them. The female—I have to find a way to label them properly. I've just been working numerically, M1, M2, F1, and so on, but it's not practical. In any case, the older female walked right up to me with no hesitation, touched the fabric of my shirt, and very quickly focused on the buttons. She flipped them over to discover the nacre on the inside. I'd never even noticed it myself. Their minds are fascinating. They like beautiful objects, art. They *sing*."

The cry grew louder for a moment, then petered out into a whine. Val couldn't make herself acknowledge it. "Them . . ." she said uselessly. He seemed to gain energy as she lost it, to pull it out of her.

"You know," he said.

She nodded.

"They're hybrids, it seems. A mixture of *sapiens* and *neanderthalensis*. Something we've never seen."

She'd seen the large, wet eyes. Neanderthal skulls had larger eye sockets—to allow them to see more clearly in the dark, some thought. And the eyes had been attached to a face, though she'd chosen not to see that. A face glimpsed only for an instant, not quite like her own.

Now, the possibility of observing how they lived, trying to communicate with them. The possibilities overwhelmed her. Mostly what stirred inside her was wonder—a pure interest in a new dimension of understanding suddenly opening up. But there was, besides this, the idea that she would be among the first. That distinction always meant something, though in a base, grasping way.

If the beings had *sapiens* in them, as George believed, other people necessarily had to have known about the population at some point and perhaps still did. But George's "we" had not meant *we who are human*, but rather *we who are developed society.*

"It was necessary to act, you understand," George pursued. "This moment, this seminal—"

The cry grew louder again, hoarse but insistent. Preoccupied, Val had stopped hearing it. Now she gave George a questioning look, but any meaning seemed to bounce off him.

"They're here . . ." she said.

George shook his head, very slightly. "As I said, there have been some unexpected developments. Contact is a delicate process. They were hesitant, of course. They couldn't remain hidden for so long without some sort of taboo on contact with us, with *sapiens*. Though it's difficult to say when this developed, I have some theories. Some tribes of the Yakuts know of them. They have stories, at least. In any case, my overtures were met with hostility when finally met at all. An initial offering desecrated. A hare's corpse left near camp once, which I worried one of you had seen. But I was breaking through, slowly. I had cameras up and drop sites where I left gifts: furs, some reels of string—all sanitized, of course. Eventually they began to accept them. Before we returned to Yakutsk I had even seen one, face-to-face, at some distance, and no aggressive moves were made." His excitement appeared slightly wild. His speech, though nearly as correct and fluent as always, hid convictions that had veered wildly, not anchored by rationality.

"But Vasiliy"—he spat the name like a curse—"wanted the project aborted. He said to hold off until a more convenient time for certain parties of interest . . . it's not important. What he really meant to do was to steal credit. To cut me out. To get *his* name—"

George was talking to himself now. Just as he seemed not to hear the terrible wail from the tree line, he seemed not to see Val. He stopped talking only when she took a small step backward.

"To cut *us* out," he amended, registering her expression.

She let out a soft laugh of horror, which only seemed to encourage him. Or perhaps there was no connection. She was not his focus.

"It's nothing to worry about. I always plan for contingencies. Or, at least, I can always find a way out."

"What happened?"

He smiled. "I had to expedite the process to work around Vasiliy. The cave is a sacred site to them. You've probably realized that already."

She had not. The cave, its overwhelming beauty and mystery, had left her mind entirely.

"They don't go often or predictably, as far as I can tell, but they lurk around it. They watch us. So I thought to open it in order to draw them out. I knew I was risking their anger, of course, but there were no other options. This is, you understand, a revelation that will fundamentally transform our concept of history and human evolution. It's only the beginning. Studying their culture will be interesting, of course. But once we can isolate the creature from the culture, so to speak, to try even to see how they interact with our world when immunized to disease and properly socialized from a young age—"

Overwhelmed by this avalanche of revelations, she had almost forgotten about the noise in the forest. Now, she heard it again with terrible clarity. "George."

"And moreover, it's my life's work."

"What did you *do*?"

"They were more upset than I'd anticipated."

"About the cave?"

He nodded. "Unwilling to be placated with gifts. But I knew the risk, of course. I returned to the cave after you'd left and met them at the mouth. There were more than I'd ever seen at once—seven in total, including the child. They work quite collaboratively, without any emphasis on gender. The leader, in fact, of this little band was a female. They took me with them through the woods. I can't begin to describe this experience. In many ways it was the culmination of my career. But I wasn't sure if they'd take me to some sort of camp or settlement—I'd never managed to find one, they're quite elusive when they choose to be—or to some clearing to kill me."

A sense of danger, of exposure to a hostile force, had been creeping up on Val throughout this conversation, and now it was too strong to ignore. The piercing noise again. He had committed an act of terrible trespass, and she was complicit.

"Let's go into my tent," she said, looking around.

He laughed a laugh bright and hot, like the embers of a cigarette unwisely flicked, landing on skin. She recoiled from it, and he looked strangely hurt for a moment. "If they want to kill you, a tent's not going to help."

"*Do* they want to kill us? Are they coming after you? After . . ." She found herself unable to directly reference the cry or what was making it.

Raking his hair back with his fingers, he paused before replying. "We have to radio, then move to the pickup spot."

"It's broken."

"No, no." He turned to walk toward the radio. Val stood still, watching him from a distance as he performed the exact same steps she and Mark had. When he reached the blank channel, he said something in Russian, just a word or two.

After a moment, a voice came on the other line. She recognized the voice as Anatoliy's, though he spoke Russian and with none of his usual easy humor. George and Anatoliy conversed in clipped, businesslike Russian for some minutes. Of the two, Anatoliy seemed more concerned. George's voice rose too, but with something closer to animation. As Val watched them, George beckoned her over.

"Where are Kit and Mark?" he asked, when she reached him. Apparently their whereabouts had not concerned him until Anatoliy had thought to ask.

She looked at him again. There was a certain tension in his shoulders that she'd never seen before. The gleam in his eyes, a fractured mirror of its usual light. She spoke slowly. "Mark went to find help. He's headed toward that farm. Kit's here. He's sick and he's lying down in his tent."

George's tensed shoulders jerked. "He's *sick*?" he responded, too loudly.

Anatoliy said something in Russian. Val heard, through it all, an encore of shrieking from the tree line. Involuntarily, she turned her head toward it. A hot hand grabbed her wrist, and she turned back to face George. His face was contorted in fury, just as it had been that day she'd followed him through the woods. But she knew the face now. It couldn't shock her like it had before, when she'd thought of him as the most coherent person she knew. She didn't respond.

"Do you realize what disease means for an isolated population? What it could mean for the work?"

Val paused, listening to the hoarse cry still breaking in from afar. "What's making that noise?"

"I thought you were ambitious, at least. I considered you a person with vision. But clearly you're incapable of seeing past your own petty preoccupation with procedure."

She reacted with a noise that might have been anything, a ragged deflation of the lungs. "You didn't think I was a person with vision. You thought I was small enough to fit through the hole at the top of the cave. And that Mark was maybe big enough to help move the rocks like those people did. Which is stupid." She began to understand only as she spoke that she'd thought it all out dozens of times in the last week. Her point didn't include Kit, and she realized she didn't really know why George had brought him. Maybe he'd seemed like a better option before he'd fought with George, and he couldn't find a way to shake him before the trip. Or maybe he just seemed easily bought. He really did have ambition, in the same way George had it.

"I thought that all of you were pliable and indecisive enough not to make waves. And that was true enough."

The wail grew louder. Val thought to go to the thing, the child—it was a baby's cry, unmistakably. But then she might kill it if she did, having spent the last day cooped up with a fever patient. George still held on to her wrist, his grip becoming painful. She yanked it away now. "You have to give it back. It will die if you don't. Or they'll kill us to get at it."

He opened his mouth but didn't respond. He was thinking, rapidly. Rage and panic passed across his face successively before he managed to restore his mask of placidity.

"What is the plan?" Anatoliy asked in English over the radio.

Ignoring him, George spoke to Val. "You'll come with me to the plane, trailing at a distance of three meters, and you'll sit as far from us as is possible on the plane, with some sort of fabric wrapped over your face and mouth—not gauze, something thick."

"And Kit? Mark?" She met his eye without any trepidation. She found herself furious.

"We'll come back for them."

"I'm not leaving Kit."

George laughed. "Die, then."

She said nothing. He took a second to assess whether she was serious in her refusal, then shook his head pityingly. She knew her voice would waver if she tried to say anything else, but she didn't break eye contact. He stood still, staring down with a flushed face, lips pressed thin, eyes gleaming furiously. The eyes, in their fractured rage, seemed to eclipse the rest of his face, to loom disembodied above her like two malicious spirits. She thought for a moment that he might hit her.

George turned away and said something to Anatoliy in Russian. The pilot responded curtly, then the radio went dead. Neither George nor Val spoke. They stood facing the trees, listening to the child in the woods. George shrugged sharply with contempt, but he didn't insult her again.

He didn't say goodbye either. He simply turned and walked away toward the tree line. She thought to follow him, but the risk of exposing the baby to disease stopped her. *You're a lunatic. You're a fool,* she thought. These might be the last words she ever spoke to him, if she spoke them out loud. Surely the group George had met would come for the child, if not for revenge. She called out instead, "Give it back!"

He didn't turn around or even break pace. He walked on boldly toward the trees with the confidence of a person who sees constellations of fate in scattered chaos.

18

By midday, Mark reached a small stream coming down from the mountains, but it was shallower than he'd hoped, hardly worth marking on a map in its current state. Perhaps it was more significant with snow melt. He tried to see if he could trace it back to the main river in order to orient himself, but this attempt proved fruitless.

The water, when he put his hand in it, was clear enough. He refilled his water bottles at the deepest point he could find, trying to avoid algae or silt. The results were still slightly cloudy in the plastic bottle. He drank from the metal bottle instead. There, at least, he couldn't see the dirt. After washing the sweat from his face and neck, he returned to the trek.

Soon after, he became aware of the sensation of being watched. He was not sure at first where this perception came from. It was purely instinctual. He didn't hear anything but his footsteps. But then, from the corner of his eye, he perceived movement behind him. Not an animal, or at least not a small one.

Sometime after George left, Val peered outside the tent. The tree line loomed above her. It reminded her of a half-unfinished jigsaw puzzle glued to a board that her father had framed and hung in their living room. Five hundred pieces, an oil painting of an evergreen forest. They'd worked on it as a family, in the last weeks of her mother's life, and lost a few pieces in the process. Her mother had broken down at one point, sobbing, saying, "I'll be dead in a month and I'm sitting around doing a jigsaw puzzle."

This was not Val's memory; it was Lily's. But she'd heard it often enough that it had taken on distinct dimensions in her mind, like a series of still photographs. She did have one memory of those months. She lay with her mother on the couch, touching her hair, a blanket over them with a soup stain at the corner. She had seen someone die, sort of, but it gave no practical insight.

Now, she lit a cigarette, turned toward the body in the sleeping bag, and asked, on an exhale, "Are you dying?"

Kit opened his eyes. They were sunken, ringed with blue, exhausted but alert. "Yes."

"*Fuck* you!" she said, and laughed. "I thought you were *dying.* I thought I was gonna be stuck here with your dead body."

"Hm."

"I mean, I knew you'd be fine. But you know."

"Sure."

"Where have you been? In your mind, I mean. What have you been dreaming about?" She realized that, in her excitement, she'd moved so close that she hovered over him. She backed away.

"My wife."

"That's nice."

"Yeah."

"I'm glad you're awake."

Val explained to him, in short, what had happened. And then, when he had some understandable questions, she explained the whole thing a few more times, in more detail than she'd expected to remember, for several hours. They weren't sure what else to do. He dwelt especially on the baby's cry. He had heard it, in his delirium, and seemed at first relieved, then disturbed, that it had not been the concoction of an overcooked brain. His body was still very weak, but his fever had broken and his rationality was restored.

"Where did he *get* it? He *stole* it?" Kit was asking, not for the first time, when a lone, terrible howl broke out from the forest—louder, closer, more desperate than they'd heard before. Val looked at Kit, and he looked at her. She turned then and grabbed her bear spray.

The first howl was met by another, then another and another, until Val could not be sure how many wolves there were. They were narrowing in on a kill, probably. On something one of them already had in its jaws. That was how it worked, she thought. But then she wasn't sure *why* she thought so or where the idea had come from. And what if she was wrong?

It would be better, still, not to move. Not to make a sound, to draw attention to herself. Unless they could smell her. Smell Kit. Knew that he was sick. Easy prey. She wanted to ask Kit what he thought, whether staying in the tent was logical or only made sense in a childish way, like the idea that monsters could get you only if you stepped out of bed or stuck a toe out from under your blanket. She couldn't get the words out.

Kit wouldn't know about wolves anyway. It wasn't the sort of thing to capture his interest. Mark would know. George too. Useless.

The terrible cries kept breaking in on her thoughts. "Let's go to the cave," she found herself saying. "In the clearing here, they can surround us. I could keep them off with bear spray if they're only coming from one direction."

"They're hunting something else near us," Kit argued.

"Like what? Mark?"

"Reindeer? Mark is probably far away. I just mean it might be wiser to do nothing."

This was punctuated by another howl.

"I don't want to sit here and do nothing."

Their discussion was brief. Kit maintained they'd draw attention to themselves. Val argued the wolves were coming already and probably smelled them, which Kit disputed. A howl broke through this, alarmingly close. Val said she was leaving anyway and taking the bear spray. Kit, after a moment, followed.

Val thought briefly that she should run in a zigzag pattern to confuse the wolves, but maybe this was only applicable to gunmen and alligators. In any case, Kit could hardly be asked to try it in his state. He couldn't afford to waste the energy. He seemed to lope rather than run, collapsing in on himself with each stride. She had to force herself not to outpace him. Her legs wanted to move faster, some awful part of her wanted to leave him to his fate, and she tried to beat this feeling down. The howls grew closer. She expected to see a wolf break through the trees at any moment but didn't see any.

They were nearly to the cave by the time they slowed down. Kit collapsed at its mouth and put his hands on his face, before dragging them slowly up through his sweat-matted hair. Silence behind them now. Val said she'd go back, very quietly, to check if the wolves were following. She made her footsteps as soft as she could and held the bear spray out in front of her, index finger on the trigger. Something stopped her from going too far, though: a fear of alerting the animals to her presence, and the insistent idea that her thoughts were disorganized, her judgment warped by the day's continued onslaught of terror and incomprehension. She wondered if she'd gotten too close, if they could hear her from where she stood.

After a minute of indecision, she unlaced her boots and pulled them off as quietly as she could before turning back. If they noticed her, this choice would surely doom her, but the necessity of totally silent retreat took precedence.

Kit said they should go in, down to where the passage narrowed. That way if the wolves followed, or anything else, they couldn't surround them—she could fend them off with the spray. In any case, it was less risky to hide than to remain exposed, even if it meant trapping themselves. They both looked at the spray. He offered to take the can himself but accepted her reasoning that she was in a better physical condition. Val relaced her boots. There was no harm in staying hidden. She didn't want to attempt to scope out the camp again. If the wolves had not come, the other threat would, soon enough.

Neither had brought a flashlight. They walked silently through the half dark, feeling their way forward along the cold, damp walls. They stopped at the end of the twilight zone, just before the passage plunged into complete darkness. The cave, it struck her, was no longer a subject to pull apart and study. Now it was again what it had been for millennia, a refuge.

She felt acutely uncomfortable, with a throat so dry it seemed to stick together, heart still pounding, muddy socks, a pebble digging into her heel. The pungent stench of adrenaline wafted from under her arms. Kit was in an even worse state. She couldn't see more than the outline of his face, straining in fear and exhaustion. For a long time he seemed as if he was about to speak but remained silent.

He sat down against the wall of the cave, and she did the same. It felt good against her back, cool and rough. The longer she sat, the more alive it seemed to her, humming against her skin. *Energetic*, as Lily would say. She thought about the Cherokee, who would write messages backward in the dark zones of caves, so the spirits could read them.

They spent some time like this. Val wasn't sure how long. She couldn't read her watch and found herself too tired to walk into the light to make out its face. Exhaustion had overtaken her. *What if we stay here forever?* she thought, leaning into the delirium, the illogic of the place. She couldn't think about the day and what had occurred. The cave seemed to thrum with the beat of her heart. Kit sat very still, perhaps asleep. She closed her eyes, deciding to do the same.

Mark realized quickly that the form was human. Fully so. And what was more, a person he knew. The dull face and noble bearing of Vasiliy Vasilievich Novikov. Dressed in hunting gear, with a large hiking backpack, he looked like he was exactly where he should be. In his element. He was reaching upward toward a tree with a knife. Mark's eyes darted up. No threats lurking in the tree. Only a small box tied to it. A camera. He was cutting it down, about to drop it into a bag.

"Vasiliy," Mark said.

The man turned, smiling. Mark hadn't startled him at all. "Hello, Mike!"

"Mark."

"Yes, of course, hello."

"What are you doing out here?" He should have asked this first. It didn't matter at that juncture whether he was Mark or Mike.

"There seems to be an emergency," he stated almost gently, "according to George."

"How is that possible? George is missing now. Or . . ."

"Or what?"

"I don't know. Gone. He left and hasn't come back. But I'm worried about him, and Val, alone with Kit, who's sick, and . . ."

"And what?"

"The camp was wrecked. Somebody came in the night and stole things. I went to get help." Was this all? He felt more afraid now. Things were not connecting. Vasiliy's ease only made the situation appear more dire. What exactly did Vasiliy know? And how? What did *Mark* know, really? Not much. He'd been presented with a facade of understanding and accepted it without a second thought.

Vasiliy took in Mark's explanation calmly. Clearly, he had come to address the problem. But why was he out here, so far away? And how could he know about George? Mark opened and closed his mouth, shutting off the urge to ask questions. Vasiliy was out here tying up some loose ends, or cutting them. Vasiliy dropped the camera into his backpack, then smiled at Mark as if they shared a secret joke.

Mark could make out the unwieldy shape of several other cameras through the tough synthetic fabric of the backpack. There had been a hint of challenge in Vasiliy's look, though Mark registered this only after the smile had disappeared.

They walked together back toward the camp, Frou Frou trotting ahead. Vasiliy said they'd reach it before the brief night, if they were efficient. He stopped every so often to cut a camera but didn't make noticeable detours. This raised more questions about the cameras. It wasn't hard to see why Vasiliy wanted to secure their evidence for himself, having broken his alliance with George, but how much area did they cover, and how thoroughly? Vasiliy couldn't cut them all down himself and wasn't making any attempt to do so. Why go so far then? He also wondered how far George had ventured during his brief disappearances throughout the dig. Surely not this far. How big was this operation? How many people knew? Mark wanted to say how strange it all was. He wanted to say so over and over again. But it seemed wiser just to walk.

Eventually a fact dawned on him that he should have realized from the start, and he couldn't help but voice it.

"You were out here looking for George."

Vasiliy nodded. "I had a theory. It proved fruitless. So we'll go back to the source."

Brightness, voices coming toward her, singing. When Val opened her eyes, she saw that the light was warm and flickering, emanating from fire. The song, a sort of moaning, quiet but nearing, sung by a chorus of voices. It echoed up and down the walls of the cave. She looked at Kit, who looked at her. She couldn't make herself turn her head to see what made the light and noise. Something deeper than rationality forbade it. Shakily she stood and lurched forward into the darkness.

They followed, at a distance, singing. She knew they must hear her, but they didn't increase their pace. Where was Kit? Had he stayed behind? He had seemed so depleted. Maybe he'd just accepted death. That was the more logical reaction. It was foolish to run. She was headed toward a dead end and knew it. Still, she found it impossible to stop. Her mind couldn't organize itself into any coherent pattern, collapsing into disconnected pieces every time she tried to think through her situation.

The voices grew louder, gaining in energy. Still, their language was soft, vowel-heavy, each alien syllable flowing into the next without pause. There was no repeating melody; it sounded instead like an ancient lyric poem, a chanting underworld chorus. As their song grew louder, it overlapped with echo so she couldn't get a sense of their number. Underneath it, footsteps and a horrible dragging noise.

The lights she and the others had so painstakingly installed had all been ripped up. How stupid, not to notice this from the start. She had been too addled to see their absence or even sense the wrongness of the place. Or else everything had felt so entirely wrong that this significant detail had blown past her unremarked, like a leaf in a storm. She stumbled, fell, cut her palms and scraped her knees, stood again, and hurried farther into the darkness. All the way, she felt along the wall with her cut palm, leaving blood. The only light in the passage came from behind, and still she could not look back.

Unrelenting, the song approached. The footsteps, the dragging. And their smell: earthy, rich, mineral, and somehow familiar. She saw the light play off the rocks still remaining in the avalanche. They were more dissembled, it seemed, than when she'd last seen them, though she didn't pause to consider it. She climbed over, into the painted chamber, hoping to find Kit there. But it was dark and empty.

Even so, she had studied its shape well enough to know where it narrowed into a passage too low and narrow to crawl through any farther. She reached this point then, feeling exposed, and turned around.

Back to the wall, she watched as the chamber filled with light. She looked up at the paintings. They were even more beautiful than she'd remembered. Sweeping lines of muscle and sinew, formed so naturally against the contours of rock. The animals seemed to move across the cave's ceiling as the light flickered, to run and to dance. The impression lasted only a moment. Silence as the singing ceased. The smell of blood was very pungent now. She felt eyes on her and finally met them with her own.

They stood at a farther distance than she'd expected to see them, huddling together closely, as if one being. Their eyes were very large and wet, widened, glistening like jelly. If children's eyes grew larger as their bodies did, this might be what they looked like. Focusing, she could make out their features. Heavy brows and sunken cheeks. Not all alike, not one huddled mass—individuals with individual faces. A variety of noses, cheeks, lips. Almost like her own, close enough that the difference felt significant. It frightened her. They stared at her with the same look of shock she must have been making herself. A wave passed back and forth, a shared feeling. And yet the nature of this feeling—terror, disbelief—also acted as a wall between them.

Her gaze traveled down. They were holding something, a heavy, unwieldy object. A human form, almost. Long elegant limbs, fabric hanging off it, a neck and jaw and, above this, nothing. A crater.

It took her a second to understand what she was looking at. It seemed unreal, more like a movie prop than anything else. Only when her mind provided a narrative explanation could she process the sight. They had bludgeoned him to death, then kept going. The whole top of the head was gone, leaving a ragged red edge, a steep angle backward. Some of the skull remained in the back, holding what looked, through the blood, like shreds of brain. The worst part was not the blood, though, or the shattered line of bone, but the absence above it.

She screamed. Cringing back trying to shrink into the wall, she covered her face with her hands, waiting for them to come for her. An ugly thud. Footsteps retreating. Then she was alone in the dark, facing the thing that couldn't be real, smelling blood.

The camp was deserted. The structures stood as ruined as they had been when Mark had left, objects strewn about. But now Kit's tent was torn ominously on one side, the rank smell of shit and wet dog permeating the air. Mark took all these details in at once—his senses felt heightened. "Wolves," Vasiliy explained, pointing at a pile of scat with the toe of his boot. He let Mark freeze, then assess the scene, before clarifying that the wolves were certainly gone.

"They're not here. Kit and Valerie, I mean," said Mark.

"So it appears."

"Do you think . . . ?"

Vasiliy shrugged.

Mark called out their names, though never raising his voice above what he'd use in a heated argument. Vasiliy went straight to what had formerly been George's tent to sift through its remnants, grabbing up various typed pages and notepads to add to his hoard of cut cameras. He managed to make this sordid scrambling into a bold and natural act. The feat reminded Mark of George.

Mark himself was relegated to a more normal and morally guided pattern of behavior, he felt, because he couldn't pull off this other way of being. But he didn't really want to be a suave, intrepid person if it meant he would also be shameless. "Kit!" he called again. "Valerie?"

There were paw prints all through the drying mud, overlaying the bare footprints he'd seen when he'd left. He noticed two fresher sets of prints in boots, leading toward the path to the cave. Vasiliy, when informed, told him to wait as he gathered what was relevant of George's trampled, mud-caked papers. After a few minutes Mark began to walk without him next to the smaller set of boot prints. He walked slowly, dreading what he might find.

"I don't know why the wolves didn't follow them. They could have tracked them easily. A wolf's nose really is a remarkable feat of evolution. But maybe they smelled other creatures too. Ones that could have posed a threat." Vasiliy had come up behind him. Mark did not reply. He was not sure why George and Vasiliy had fallen out in Yakutsk, but no lingering loyalty caused Mark's reserve now. It was Vasiliy's light, almost ironic demeanor in the realm of unknown horrors that put him on his guard. He could tell his companion was enjoying himself.

They followed the footprints to the mouth of the cave. The markings were very light on the mostly resolidified ground, almost ghostly. This whole catastrophe, he thought, came from following ghosts. Still, he felt himself compelled forward. A figure sat at the mouth of the cave, slim and straight. It stood as they came into view.

"Mark," said Kit. Behind him sat Valerie. She stood too now.

Mark could almost laugh with relief. Both alive. He pushed the question of George out of his mind as he clapped Kit on the shoulder. "You're alive."

Kit seemed to stare through him, then flashed a smile. "*You're* alive."

Valerie walked forward. Like Kit, she had a strange look on her face, but she said it was wonderful to see him safe. Circumstantially, it was almost impossible for her to be making fun of him. As he began to say it was wonderful to see her too, he saw that she and Kit were already turned to focus on Vasiliy.

"I ran into him," said Mark.

"Anatoliy told me there was a situation emerging and that it wasn't safe," Vasiliy added.

"Is that what he told you?" Kit's face betrayed a look that always made Mark uncomfortable. A look that said he was both near and far away, a participant and an observer at the same time. It seemed less intentional now than it had in the past.

"George is dead," said Valerie. "He's in the cave. They killed him and put him in the cave."

An awful silence followed. George wasn't the sort of person who simply died. It was ridiculous. Even Vasiliy looked stunned, though quickly he collected himself and asked, "You saw this occur?"

"I saw the body."

"But they've left?"

"Yes," said Kit finally. He'd seen it too, of course.

Without another word, Vasiliy dug his flashlight out and walked into the cave. Nobody followed. He returned some minutes later, looking slightly paler. In the interim, Mark explained about the cameras, his suspicions. In turn, he was told an extraordinary tale of bloodthirsty wolves, chanting Neanderthals, ritual murder. They were only halfway through when Vasiliy emerged, and they repeated it all from the start as they walked down to what had been their camp. Valerie did most of the talking, her voice eerily mechanical. Kit, fatigued, only added occasional clarifications. He'd been in the twilight zone and seen the beings in more detail. Vasiliy had questions about their number and subsequent movements that Kit and Valerie couldn't answer.

Vasiliy had a small, portable satellite phone in a side pocket of his backpack, a hypermodern contraption none of them had ever seen before. It was smaller than his head and couldn't have weighed more than two pounds. He used it to communicate with Anatoliy, who had flown him in at a distance in order to cut the cameras. As Vasiliy had worked his way inward toward the camp, Anatoliy had flown in to wait for him there. All of this, Mark deduced—Vasiliy spoke quickly in Russian into his portable phone and explained nothing. After surveying the camp one last time, he led them to Anatoliy in a dazed, dehydrated procession. Mark wondered briefly if Vasiliy would shoot them all at close range once he'd corralled them into the plane. *Well,* said a voice in his head, *it is what it is*. This was Valerie's apathetic voice, unexpectedly useful now.

When they reached the plane, Anatoliy was grim. Vasiliy tried to make some joke to him in Russian, and he responded flatly. He was gentler with the Canadians, asking them all if they were hurt before guiding them onto the plane. It was surprising to see him work so calmly and efficiently, a jovial personality forced to adapt to grave circumstances. He handled it well, Mark had to admit.

"You called him after talking to George?" Valerie asked Anatoliy, when he reached her. Vasiliy was already inside the plane, as was Kit.

Anatoliy paused for a second, then spoke carefully. "This is a thing I've seen in the air force. Somebody not making sense like this. Going from their mind."

Valerie nodded and thanked him for coming, which prompted Mark to do the same. They left the Malova Valley in silence. Mark was the only one who even looked out the window to watch the trees and mountains grow smaller. The others sat straight in their chairs, faces unreadable. The view was beautiful, but he didn't feel much.

He thought back to what Vasiliy's wife had said about the place. Kit had repeated her words to him, once. *Occupied.* This was no place for them. They'd stepped on a very old land mine. He knew there was more to consider, that a tangled mess awaited him in Yakutsk. Explanations to be made to the university. Stories nobody would believe. Investigations. An inquest, maybe. The body was still there, in the cave. He couldn't make himself think anymore. George was dead. Skull bashed in. Brains leaking out. (Valerie had been descriptive on this point, though quiet and monotone in delivery.) Mark easily could have joined him in this fate. He had nearly died. He had learned such wonderful things. Been so close to something almost unimaginable. A knowledge that had changed him, that could change everything else in the world. The biggest thing he'd ever live through, he knew.

His mind was exhausted. His body too. His head throbbed. His legs and feet hurt. His back strained, and the muscles between his ribs were wincing in toward his heart. Everything about him ached together in a thumping rhythm. The trees blurred into something liquid—a gray-green broth with little pointed tips bubbling up. He closed his eyes.

19

Vasiliy drove them all back to his house. Nobody questioned this out loud. They took turns showering immediately upon arrival—all smelled quite strongly from the pungent sweat produced by fear, and in Kit's case this was complemented by the aroma of stomach acid. Once clean, Kit went to the guest room he shared with Mark to lie down.

He was roused by Tuskulaana to join the others for lunch the next day. He didn't ask how long he'd slept nor did he attempt to do the math in his head. Over a heavy meat stew that, in their current state, none but Mark could quite stomach, Vasiliy presented them with definitive next steps.

First, the facts. George was dead. His body lay decomposing in a cave, unless those creatures had moved it. They had no plausible explanation for his death. The truth was not plausible.

"What about the cameras?" Val asked, betraying no emotion.

Vasiliy did not have to pause before replying, "Broken. They smashed them all."

Mark set down his soupspoon.

"There is no proof," Vasiliy continued. "The police will not expend resources to investigate the claim that a caveman killed your thesis adviser."

Nonetheless, Kit, Val, and Mark were simple graduate students, innocent in all that went awry, so Vasiliy felt some responsibility to extricate them from the situation. And as the truth was implausible, it had become necessary to agree on a more reasonable lie.

What had happened, then, was simple: George had killed himself. He left a note. He had debts, a broken marriage, an eventful but controversial academic career, and now a failed excavation.

"The body," said Kit. "A person can't do that to himself." He was a little disturbed at his own pragmatism, but it was true. Even the most enterprising depressive would find it difficult to bludgeon himself to death, to remove the top of his head. Val looked at Kit with concern.

"Don't worry about it," Vasiliy replied. There were people involved in this, it didn't hurt to say now, who would prefer the endeavor be paused and resumed at a later date. And for this specific chapter to be closed neatly and permanently.

"I want the needle," Kit found himself saying.

Val made a noise of bitter surprise but did not argue. Mark shifted in his seat.

Vasiliy leaned back in his chair. "You don't seem to understand your position. You went into the woods with three other people and left with two. I'll take care of it for you, but you need to say what I tell you to say and nothing more. Then you need to leave and pretend it never happened." He paused, taking in their faces, then added more softly, "It's not often that you get the chance to do that, to erase mistakes. Take it as a gift and move on."

Tuskulaana came in then, holding a pot of tea and four cups on a tray. Kit wondered how long she'd been lingering by the door. Everyone was always creeping around, listening in, sneaking and spying. He missed his wife. She was always direct.

"Do you understand?" asked Vasiliy.

Tuskulaana poured Kit a cup of tea. He ignored her, locking eyes with Vasiliy. Min-Seo would have kicked him under the table for this behavior. "What are you going to do with it then? The needle."

"It's safe."

Kit and Vasiliy regarded each other. There was no leverage, he realized. And really, hadn't he brought it on himself? He'd known it was all wrong from the start. He'd ignored his own reason at every turn in deference to ambition. He'd flouted protocol, dismissed his commitment to doing good work, just to chase something too big to catch.

He thought of the impossible procession he'd seen in the cave, while still recovering from his delirium. Their unlikely eyes, gorgeous in the half-light; their heavy brows and gliding movements. Their low, hypnotic song. The corpse they pulled along. He thought of his wife, who had always understood the world better than he did. Their child, whom he'd held for the first time in a daze. The downy wisps of hair on his head, his skin so thin the veins showed through. A child who wasn't balancing. He thought of the three of them together. This image displayed itself on a much smaller scale than the scene in the cave. A young family was a small thing, really, and delicate. He nodded at Vasiliy and stood to leave.

Val found Vasiliy outside, trying to teach his son to play fetch with the dog. The sky, gray that morning, had cleared. The sun shone high and bright, and the flowering weeds of the field strained up toward it. Its rays passed through the leaves and petals, lighting each one as it did. The whole field seemed to glow as a result, shining, reaching up in one unified movement, a living field of Elysium. Through this, the man threw his stick and the dog cut her path. The little boy couldn't throw yet, of course, but he found his observations of the process of tossing and retrieving highly amusing.

As Vasya giggled, Val stood on the steps and watched as Frou Frou dutifully ambled back with the stick. "I thought you said she wasn't friendly."

Vasiliy glanced back at her only briefly. "Not to outsiders."

The child extracted the saliva-soaked stick from the animal's mouth, flung it to the ground, and looked up expectantly at his father. The man picked it up by the dry end and threw it again. He would continue to ignore her if she didn't press the issue.

"I don't think people will believe it. That he killed himself. He's not the type."

"They say you can't tell. I've observed that people who tend toward extremes in emotion and action are most susceptible to suicide. George certainly tended toward extremes."

She didn't like to hear George's name, especially from Vasiliy's mouth, but what he said made some sense. "Well."

Little Vasya had given up attempting to throw Frou Frou her stick, instead resorting to burying his face in her fur. Vasiliy left him to this task and moved to stand by Val on the steps.

"Are you going to bury him?"

Vasiliy smiled, though no joy was conveyed. It might have been a malicious smile or a sad one. "Yes. He'll be buried."

She could see what he was thinking: that she had been in love with George. She wanted to say, *I wasn't in love with him*, but that was the sort of thing people only said when they actually had been in love. It was true, though. She hadn't loved him. Or, at least, she couldn't remember loving him. She could think only of his body, spotlit in the dark. The unnatural contours of his ruined face; the place where his skull had been bashed into his brain. A lifetime's worth of knowledge, an exceptional intelligence—pulped by a rock. It had looked more like a movie prop than a person she'd known. And when they'd gone, stepping over his ruined body in the dark. Smelling it, feeling the last of its warmth leave it. Though she couldn't see a thing, she'd been able to sense it somehow, enough to avoid touching it. And after she'd passed it, she had run.

"He was a fool," said Vasiliy.

"Not so pragmatic as you, anyway."

"Though he was good at pretending."

"Yes."

"Until he wasn't."

"Is this supposed to be comforting?"

Vasiliy laughed. He looked her up and down, as if trying to understand the appeal, before deciding such things were beyond him. "No."

Frou Frou rolled onto her back and Vasya clapped, delighted. Vasiliy gave Val an ironic smile and waved as if to dismiss her.

"Do really bury him. Don't just say you will." She spoke with a burst of pathos, though she was speaking with a man as impassive as a gravestone.

He nodded, and she couldn't help but find it all funny. The absurdity and horror and grand, stifled emotion of it all reached their boiling point and evaporated into something hysterical. Nitrous oxide, maybe. Well, it was always the way. Whenever she felt anything strongly enough about anything, humor came to save her. "Do it," she said, "or he'll haunt you."

He shrugged. "Ghosts don't work on me."

She laughed again, and the laugh said, *You're the fool.* He smiled, comprehending but unconcerned—the feeling was mutual and mutually understood. The child began to crawl out into the sun-drenched field, and Val turned to go back into the house.

⚘

Mark had never been a good liar. His face would go red. His hands would lie dead in his lap or else flail wildly, and he'd overemphasize every word. Or so he'd been told. He was glad for the excuses of shock and exhaustion, both of which he was genuinely experiencing, to explain his behavior. Still, it seemed so unlikely that he'd managed to pull one over on Vasiliy, an impeccable liar and detector of lies. He hadn't been confronted directly, though. As long as he wasn't confronted directly, he could keep himself together. Keeping to himself, saying very little, he would run down the clock until they escaped back to Toronto. Their passage home would be rebooked for the first flight available, Vasiliy said, as soon as they confirmed the Yakutsk police wouldn't detain them—which, Vasiliy assured them, they would not.

There was no fuss about a train this time. Yakutsk had a commercial airport. This fact galled Mark; despite everything he'd experienced, his humiliation on the train still stung. But it was just like George to have left this detail out and just like Mark not to question it. As an Alaskan, he should have realized that a place like Yakutsk needed a real airport if he'd thought about it even for a second.

The fact was Vasiliy wanted them gone as soon as possible. This played to Mark's advantage. And yet he couldn't help but wait for some big reveal. A scene in which Vasiliy announced he'd known the whole time—he'd seen him steal it and was now just toying with him like a sadistic house cat. He'd been crazy to take it. He couldn't understand what had come over him. Some spirit of heroism, maybe. Replaying it now, it was hard to believe he'd done it. On their trek back to camp, Vasiliy had walked some distance into the woods to relieve himself. He had peed in front of Mark a number of times with bewildering relish, but nobody could look dignified taking a shit. Unexpectedly, Vasiliy had left his backpack, taking only a pack of wet wipes. So, without thinking, Mark had unzipped it and taken out a camera, stashing it away in his own backpack.

Later, as they walked together in near silence, he became convinced Vasiliy knew or would soon know. That it was some kind of test, or that, at the very least, Vasiliy was surely keeping track of the number of cameras he'd recovered. But Vasiliy never confronted Mark, and the camera never disappeared from its hiding place in his backpack, wrapped in a sweat-stained undershirt, though he hadn't taken it out to check. There was always the possibility of cameras hidden in lamps. Though he wasn't sure that any such technology existed outside of spy movies, it couldn't hurt to be careful. Still, he found opportunities to covertly feel its shape while retrieving other items from the backpack. It remained where it was.

He wasn't sure the camera even contained any footage of the beings. He had never seen them, and part of him felt a burning jealousy toward Kit and Valerie, despite their thousand-yard stares when he'd found them, for having had such an opportunity. If his camera had useful footage, it would be his first look.

People would call it a hoax, he knew. Those who believed him would probably be Sasquatch enthusiasts. But it was something. Proof to himself, at least, that it had happened. And that he hadn't just *let* it happen—he'd done something. A gesture toward agency, toward truth. And if circumstances aligned, it could be more than that. If he could convince the right people to at least try to prove him wrong, they'd see what he had not yet seen in person, and it could change everything.

Kit was off brooding, so Mark was alone in the room. He lay down in bed, curling himself around the backpack like a lover.

Val went to find Kit. She needed to interact with someone sympathetic after her encounter with Vasiliy. Kit was standing in the empty road out front, smoking. She joined him there, and he handed her a cigarette. They smoked together in silence under the vast, bright, indifferent sky. Relations between them were stiff again. There was no ill will, but it was hard to know what to say.

"I'm not even enjoying this," said Val. "I think the idea of the cigarette is better than the thing itself."

Kit nodded but did not reply. She tried again.

"Waiting to get neutralized?"

"By you?"

"Who knows? Maybe I've been the spy all along. Or maybe it's you."

"Doug from the train thought we were both CIA, you know."

Even now, she found herself defaulting to a playful way of speaking. It was as good a way of surviving as any other, and she could admit she was flirtatious by nature. It was a flirtation to do with the intentional flouting of social conventions, and she did it without motive to everybody, regardless of age, gender, or context. She had learned later than was usual what the purpose of these social conventions was, and by the time she could fully value their protections, her personality was more or less set.

It was a trait Kit had always appreciated and shared, to a less pathological extent. If conversation was like a tennis game, Kit was an excellent player, whereas Mark would invariably watch the ball fly past his head, and Vasiliy was of the rare and disquieting disposition to catch it with a clenched fist, set it carefully on the ground, and stare you down, daring you to hop the net and retrieve it yourself. Val inhaled sharply, then coughed a little like a teenager.

Kit observed this with fatigued tranquility. "You're not the spy."

"No." She studied his face: eye sockets hollowed out, skin tanned without vitality. She had the impulse to pat him on the back like a hockey coach after a bad game, but resisted. "Anyway, I hope you're feeling better."

"Yeah. I'm good." He said this reflexively before elaborating. "I'm really ready to go home. I just want to see my family. I want to hold my son."

Val nodded, imagining Kit with his beautiful wife, the fat-cheeked little baby. Though he'd never spoken much of it before—or not to her, at least—he'd built a life for himself. Maybe she should do the same. She tried to picture herself married with a fat little baby but quickly erased the image. Grotesque. Still, the broader concept appealed to her, and there had to be other ways to build a life. To love mutually, giving good things and getting them in return. To connect with other people in a way that made her care about herself more.

She thought then of the baby shrieking from the tree line, of the big wet eyes in the firelight. Not for the first time, she wondered what would happen to them. Vasiliy wasn't trying to protect them, but maybe he was doing so inadvertently. Keeping them hidden, away from enterprising characters. Still, it couldn't last forever. The world was growing exponentially smaller and more connected, its mystery moving from the realm of discovery to that of invention. Inevitably, their existence would be revealed.

She felt she had a moral obligation to protect them, though any semblance of a plan eluded her. She could think through only the first few steps. She would say whatever was required to get out of Yakutsk. She would get home, and she'd find people to advise her. Nature conservationists, maybe. People in the government. Kit and Mark would corroborate her story, she assumed. But then, people did all sorts of things. Kit was in some ways a careerist. He might want to shake the whole ordeal off. And Mark had not actually seen the creatures. The university would expect answers. Maybe the police too. George's family, if he even had any living relatives. How strange that she didn't know. Her involvement with him would likely be exposed, or at least suspected. Their methods would be questioned more broadly, and she didn't feel she could defend them. The more she considered it, the more it all fell apart.

Well. She would get safely out of Yakutsk first.

"These things are really bad for you," she said, tossing her half-smoked cigarette and grinding it under her shoe. "We should quit."

Kit laughed.

That night, Val dreamed of George, dead. In the depths of the cave, she laid his body out and buried him ceremonially, trowel against his heart like an ancient warrior's sword. Once in the ground, he stirred, deciding to make the best of death. He used his trowel to dig down deeper and deeper into the earth, finding great treasures and adorning himself with them. A garnet necklace, a yellow-gold death mask like the one Schliemann had named for Agamemnon. Eventually he hit a patch of loose soil and fell through it. Sitting there in the dark, he tried to figure out if he'd landed in a hole or a tunnel.

ACKNOWLEDGMENTS

Though writing is usually a solitary pursuit, making a book is not. I'd like to thank those who contributed to *The Sleeping Land* both directly and indirectly.

To my agent, Zeynep Sen, who supported me through the process of writing my first draft, then worked tirelessly to find it a home.

To my editor, Chris Heiser, whose expertise, eye for structure, and attention to detail brought out the best in the book.

To the team at Unnamed Press for all the care they took with the book, including Brandon Taylor for acquiring the manuscript, Allison Woodnutt for helping with publicity, and Jaya Nicely for designing such an evocative cover.

To Tess Malova—without her knowledge of Russian language and culture, this book would never have made it past the first few chapters.

To my draft readers, Tamar Sholev and Dorian Lee, for giving such insightful feedback and the occasional ego boost when needed.

To those who thoughtfully advised on various practical points, including Keren Levine, Maayan Levine, and Chun Ying Wang.

To my coworking friends, Alex Kovner and Ceri Savage, along with the Berlin Shut Up and Write community, for keeping me focused throughout the writing and editing of the book.

To my wonderful friends who supported me through this process: Visar Houter, Alex Millar, Emma Popkin, Rebecca Sell, Zack Weiner, Aerin Wilmanns, my brother, Jordan Alexander, and especially Lisa Vogel, whose kindness and generosity helped me find a home in this world.

To Mom and Dad, with love and gratitude. Thank you so much for everything.

www.ingramcontent.com/pod-product-compliance
Lightning Source LLC
Chambersburg PA
CBHW020334310726
48979CB00015B/2368/J
9781961884199